bartolomé

The Infanta's Pet

Little Island received financial assistance from
The Arts Council (An Chomhairle Ealaíon), Dublin, Ireland.

Little Island gratefully received financial assistance from
Bundesministerium für Unterricht, Kunst und Kultur, Vienna.

The Publisher acknowledges the financial assistance of
Ireland Literature Exchange (translation fund), Dublin, Ireland.
www.irelandliterature.com   info@irelandliterature.com

The publication of this work was supported by
a grant from the Goethe-Institut, which is funded
by the German Ministry of Foreign Affairs.

BARTOLOMÉ
THE INFANTA'S PET

by
Rachel Van Kooij

Translated by
Siobhán Parkinson

BARTOLOMÉ: THE INFANTA'S PET

Published 2012 by Little Island,
7 Kenilworth Park,
Dublin 6W, Ireland,
www.littleisland.ie

First published as *Kein Hundeleben für Bartolomé*
by Jungbrunnen Verlag in Vienna in 2003

ISBN 978-1-908195-26-5

British Library Cataloguing Data. A CIP catalogue record
for this book is available from the British Library.

Cover design by Someday
Typesetting by Kieran Nolan
Printed in Poland by Drukarnia Skleniarz

10 9 8 7 6 5 4 3 2

Part 1

Bartolomé

FROM a distance, with its low white-washed houses, the village looked like a smudge of white that an artist had painted between the greeny-brown of the hills.

Bartolomé Carrasco was sitting in the shade on the crumbling old steps of the church, watching the children who gathered here every evening after supper to play on the village square. They were barefoot, like himself, and not well dressed.

Bartolomé was drawing in the dust with his finger. He was sketching his thirteen-year-old brother, Joaquín, who was kicking a ball around with his friends. The ball was really a pig's bladder, filled tight as a drum with air and wrapped in rags. Now that the sun had gone down, it was not as hot as it had been, and the game was fast and furious. Children's voices echoed hoarsely over the square. Dust swirled around the players.

One of them gave the ball a mighty kick, and it came rolling in Bartolomé's direction. It looked as if it was going to ruin his drawing. He hauled himself up to kick it out of the way with his club foot, but he couldn't manage it, and instead he went head over heels into the sand, and the ball landed on his hump. Above him, he could hear the laughter of the children. Joaquín grabbed him by the scruff of the neck and pulled him up, shook him like a ragdoll so that sand came streaming out of his shirt and trousers, and shoved him roughly back onto the steps.

3

'Give it over,' he muttered to Bartolomé.

A whisper went around among the children: 'The cripple wants to play.' They didn't dare say it out loud, though, because anyone who made fun of the ugly little dwarf would have Joaquín to reckon with.

The game went on, more furiously than before. It pained Bartolomé to watch. Joaquín was the quickest and most skilful. Time and again, he used his long legs to keep possession of the ball.

Those legs! thought Bartolomé enviously. His own legs were spindly little sticks, out of which grew feet like two squashed lumps of clay with crooked toes. He certainly couldn't run on them. Even walking was difficult, more like stumbling. His arms were far too long in comparison with his legs and his body with its big hump, but if he balanced on his hands he could scramble along quite quickly, like an animal, on all fours. But he mustn't let anyone see, or he'd be beaten. Not by his father, Juan, but by his mother, Isabel.

Juan Carrasco was coachman to the little princess, the Infanta Margarita, in Madrid, and he rarely made the hard three-day journey home to visit. Most of the men of the village worked away from home. They were mostly labourers on the farms of rich landowners. Not so Juan. He had had the nerve and the determination to go to Madrid. At first he'd worked as a stable hand in the royal stables, and so good was he with horses that he came to the attention of the stable manager and was promoted to coachman.

Juan was ambitious. At first he was just an ordinary coachman, driving the luggage cart when the king journeyed from one royal castle to another. Bartolomé knew all their names. Alcázar and Buen Retiro were the city palaces. El Escorial was an abbey, Torre de la Parada a hunting lodge. Juan Carrasco, a simple country man, was soon made coachman to the Infanta, the king's little daughter. He was called Don Carrasco now in the village, and although he never came home on horseback in his fancy uniform, but came on foot and dressed like one of them, still he was hailed as a gentleman.

No, it was not his fine father who punished Bartolomé when he went creeping along on the ground. He knew what a dreadful way to behave this must be, since his own mother beat him for doing it. 'You are not an animal!' she yelled at him every time she caught him crawling. 'You are a human being, like us.'

But Bartolomé knew all too well that this was not true. He was not like his brothers and sisters. He did not have the fine upright stance of his fourteen-year-old sister Ana or the lithe limbs of Joaquín. Even though he was ten years old, he was smaller than his six-year-old sister Beatríz, and even his baby brother Manuel had a perfect body. Bartolomé was secretly jealous of the healthy skin, the straight limbs and the perfect little feet, each with five rosy toes, that he saw when his mother washed and changed the baby. Why, Bartolomé wondered, had he been born so deformed?

The football game was slowing down now. The ball was left lying on the sand. The children were tired. They'd been herding goats since early morning or pulling weeds in the miserable fields. All the work of the village fell on the shoulders of the women and children. They watered the stony fields, they looked after the olive groves and the orange and lemon orchards. Only Bartolomé and the old priest spent their days in idleness. Though, mind you, Father Rodriguez did say mass and baptised children, heard confessions and buried the dead. Bartolomé, on the other hand, could only sit and watch life passing him by.

At ten years of age, he was the only boy in the village who had never stripped off and swum in the river or gone fishing there. He'd never harvested olives or picked stones out of the fields at ploughing time. He was good for nothing.

He looked over at his sister. Beatríz was sitting happily at the front door, playing with her doll. It was just a piece of wood that she'd tenderly wrapped up in a cloth. She was rocking the doll and singing a song to her. Bartolomé knew that inside the house his mother was singing Manuel to sleep with the same song. His other sister, Ana, was sitting with the big girls by the well. They were brushing each other's hair. She was still a girl, but soon she and her friends would put on long skirts and marry. On his last visit home, Juan Carrasco had brought a suitor for his eldest daughter, a quiet, serious young man, the son of a friend. But nothing had come of it. Bartolomé had overheard his parents discussing the matter. He often lay awake at night, because his legs hurt, and that's how he'd come to overhear the conversation.

'He thinks she might give birth to another cripple.' His father's hard, accusing voice still rang in Bartolomé's ears.

'I've got four strong, healthy children,' his mother whispered. 'That's more than most.'

But that counted for nothing with the suitor, Bartolomé thought sadly, nor with his father.

As the pale red sun sank behind the houses, the children disappeared. Bartolomé waited patiently until the square had emptied. Then he looked carefully around. Most of the shutters had already been closed. He couldn't see anyone watching him. Quickly, he lowered himself onto his hands and ran like a dog. He didn't haul himself up onto his feet until he had reached the front door, and then he lurched into the house.

Homecoming

'PAPA is here!'

Beatríz came running, whooping, into the house. It was the afternoon of the following day. Isabel yanked off her apron, picked Manuel up off the floor, and positioned herself in the doorway.

Beatríz was quite right. Juan Carrasco had come home on a visit. Isabel gave a puzzled frown when she saw him. How come he'd brought a donkey and cart?

Joaquín and Ana came running from the fields, where they had been pulling weeds. Joaquín was leading the donkey now, and Ana was holding her father's hand. They came across the village square, the three of them together.

Isabel stood aside to let Juan enter. He didn't hug her until he'd got inside the room. Manuel looked suspiciously at his father. But Juan smiled at the child, took him in his strong arms and raised him up to the ceiling. For a moment, Manuel looked as if he was going to cry. Isabel kept an anxious eye on her youngest son. But in the end he plumped for laughter. Juan whirled him through the air, like a bird, and Manuel roared with pleasure. Beatríz clung jealously to Juan's legs. When Manuel was safely back in his mother's arms, Juan bent down and kissed Beatríz on her thick black curls, and he got an affectionate smack on the cheek.

Joaquín had been tying up the donkey and giving it water. He came in now, and Juan gave him a clap on the back.

Bartolomé was making himself as small as possible in the gap between the bed and the blanket chest. Isabel spotted him and pulled him out.

'Say hello to your father, Bartolomé,' she ordered. She held him tight, so that he could stand almost straight. Bartolomé hung his head.

'Hello, Papa,' he mumbled.

Juan nodded at him.

Bartolomé slipped out of his mother's grip and crept back into his corner. Joaquín pushed his way in between his parents. 'Why have you brought a donkey and cart?' he asked curiously. 'Are we rich now?'

Juan laughed hoarsely. The dust of the road made his throat rasp. 'In Madrid, every poor wretch has a donkey and cart. The rich people there have horse-drawn coaches.'

'But do they belong to us?'

For Joaquín, owning a donkey and cart was unimaginable wealth. Only the village priest, Father Rodriguez, owned a donkey, and nobody had a proper cart. They got by with handcarts. There were plenty of children to pull those, and anyone who had saved a bit of money preferred to spend it on a goat. A goat gave milk, its flesh was edible and you could make all sorts of useful things out of the hide. A donkey was a luxury.

'Pipe down, Joaquín,' Isabel rebuked her eldest son. She knew how short-tempered her husband could be when he arrived home from the long journey, tired, hungry and thirsty.

'Leave him be,' said Juan good-naturedly, sitting down on the bed. 'Just get me something to drink from Tomáz, and if Beatríz will pull off my boots for me and Ana will bring me a basin of water to wash in, I'll tell you my big news later.'

He gave Joaquín a coin, and the boy snatched a jug and was gone, as fast as his legs would carry him. Tomáz Gasset lived on the edge of the village. He had a small vineyard, and he'd set up a wine stall in his yard, with a couple of tables. Most evenings, he stood at his door with a wineskin, waiting for customers. But it was afternoon now, and he was taking a nap. Joaquín stormed into the house and woke him up unceremoniously.

'Papa's come home,' he explained, as Tomáz filled the jug with wine. 'He's come like a *señor*, a rich man,' he said boastfully, 'with a donkey and cart.'

'Well, well,' said Tomáz. 'He'll drop by here this evening, then, I suppose.'

'He surely will, Señor Gasset.'

At home, Bartolomé was watching as Beatríz pulled off her father's boots, and as Ana bathed his swollen red feet in cool water and dried them with a soft towel. Even little Manuel was able to help Juan Carrasco feel better after his strenuous journey. Isabel had planted tobacco in the spring, and she'd dried the leaves carefully, chopped them up and stuffed them into a little sack. She pressed the little sack into Manuel's hand now and pushed him towards his father. 'Take the tobacco to your father,' she ordered, and Manuel wobbled over to his father on his little legs with his arms outstretched.

'He's learnt to walk,' said Isabel proudly, as Juan pulled his youngest son on to his lap.

'Can you give Papa the pipe too, out of its bag?' he asked softly.

Juan opened the leather pouch that he carried on his belt. Manuel stuck his hand in and pulled out an old pipe with a chewed mouthpiece.

'There!' he crowed, sticking the pipe in his own little mouth.

9

Juan gave a loud laugh. 'That's my boy!' he cried.

Joaquín came running in, holding a hand protectively over the top of the wine jug, so that not a drop of wine should spill. He gave it to his father.

'Who'll bring me my mug? Or is the Infanta's coachman going to have to drink out of the jug, like a common labourer?' asked Juan.

The children watched him expectantly. Nobody moved. Which of them would be entrusted with the task of bringing him his mug?

It should be my turn now, thought Bartolomé. *I could bring him the mug. If I could just push my high chair over to the cupboard, and if I could climb up and support myself on one hand, and with the other, I could take down the mug, if I ...*

There were too many ifs. His father would never ask him to do such a thing. But his mother might think of it. He came out of his corner and tried to signal quietly to her to pass the mug quickly to him. Then he could easily manage the last few steps to his father, with the mug in his hand.

Isabel took the heavy pewter mug down from the cupboard, but instead of passing it to her dwarf son, she reached across the heads of the children with it, and gave it to her husband herself.

'Take it,' she urged him. 'Drink.' She was just as impatient to hear why he had brought a donkey and cart from Madrid as Joaquín was.

Madrid

'WE'RE moving to Madrid,' announced Juan, delighted with himself, after he'd drunk his mug of wine in one long, thirsty draught.

To Madrid! Bartolomé's eyes widened in surprise. Madrid was the king's city. It was huge. It was full of palaces where princes and princesses ate off golden plates and drank from cut-crystal glasses. The streets were thronged with horses and coaches, soldiers in uniform, all kinds of tradesmen, corner boys and beggars. There were rows upon countless rows of shops and warehouses and bars lining the narrow streets and alleys. On his visits home, their father had often described the lively doings of all these people in this fabulous city with its stately buildings. Ana, Joaquín, Bartolomé and Beatríz had listened to him, their mouths hanging open. Now they were going to move there and see it all with their own eyes.

'In recognition of my loyal service, the court high marshal has given me permission to come and get you. I was able to hire the donkey and cart cheaply. Tomorrow we'll pack up the bed, the table, the chairs and the chests and all our belongings – and off we go!'

Juan looked around. It was clear from their faces that Joaquín and Ana were delighted. Beatríz was staring at him as if he were the king himself. Manuel was too small to understand the

11

wonderful thing that Juan Carrasco had achieved. He, the son of a poor peasant, had managed to be employed at court, and now he was one of very few underlings to be allowed to bring his family to join him.

'To Madrid!' whispered Isabel. She'd never thought such a thing could happen. How could she go with the children to Madrid and leave everything behind? The house, the vegetable garden, their olive trees, the goats and the stony fields? She'd lived all her life in this little village.

'Can I tell everyone, Papa?' asked Joaquín. He'd been aware for some time that his friends were waiting for him out on the village square.

Juan nodded, and Joaquín ran out. Ana followed him to the door. None of her friends had ever left the village, and she was about to move to the fabulous city of rich princes and brave heroes.

Isabel pushed Beatríz and Manuel out into the open air as well. She had questions to ask that were not for children to hear.

In his corner, Bartolomé made himself even smaller. For the first time in his life, he hoped that his parents wouldn't notice him. If he listened, he could impress Joaquín later with his information. He'd make his brother promise, in return, to carry him through the streets of Madrid on his back, so that he could see for himself all the wonders of the city.

Bartolomé crawled under the bed. It wasn't really necessary. Isabel was so distracted, she never gave him so much as a thought.

'What about the house?' she asked. 'We can't just leave it empty.'

'I'm going to settle that this evening,' said Juan calmly. 'Tomáz has been wanting to have a proper tavern on the village square for ages.'

'He hasn't got the money to rent a house!'

'I know. So he'll have to do me a favour instead.'

'What kind of a favour?'

'He'll have to look after Bartolomé.'

'Bartolomé!' The blood drained from Isabel's face, as it did from Bartolomé's, where he was hiding under the bed.

'We can't take him with us,' Juan explained quickly. 'You told me yourself, the last time I came home, what happens when a stranger sees him. Ana is going to need a husband soon. She's clever and pretty and strong. She'll make a good match in Madrid. With a bit of luck, she could even marry a merchant or a master craftsman. And I need to find an apprenticeship for Joaquín. But the masters don't take on just anyone. They demand good money. And if Bartolomé stays on here with Tomáz, that's one less mouth to feed in Madrid.

Under the bed, Bartolomé reddened with shame and anger. How could his father talk about him as if he were not his son but some worthless object!

'But he's our son too!' cried Isabel loudly. She knew that Juan disliked Bartolomé, even if he wouldn't admit it.

Juan looked his wife in the eye. Why did she love this particular child so much?

'I know that,' he said. 'But he'll be better off with Tomáz than in Madrid. Cripples are forced to beg at the church gates there. People trample on them and jeer them.'

'But we wouldn't let that happen,' protested Isabel.

'Some day we'll be old, and then we wouldn't be able to protect him. And we can't ask Joaquín to take on such a responsibility. With Tomáz, he can make himself useful in the tavern. Tomáz has no children of his own. He'll get fond of

Bartolomé and he'll soon think of him as his own son,' said Juan, but his voice had a hard edge to it. Isabel should be sensible, he told her.

'It would break my heart to leave him behind. He's still so small.'

'He's ten years old. At that age, Joaquín was already herding the goats. You have to think of your other, healthy children now. You can't spoil their chances of a better life.' Juan stood up from the bed and took Isabel in his arms. 'This is the best way, believe me,' he said reassuringly.

Bartolomé was listening, waiting for his mother to fight his corner. He wanted to go to Madrid with the others. Tomáz would work him like a slave and would make no allowances for his poor, weak, crooked body. Bartolomé went rigid with fear. Why didn't his mother say something?

In the end, he couldn't stand it any longer. He crawled out from under the bed, pulled himself up on a chest and screeched like an abandoned young goat for his mother. Tears streamed down his face. Isabel pulled out of Juan's embrace and ran to her son. She knelt down in front of him, trying to dry his tears with the corner of her apron.

'He heard it all,' she stammered.

Juan turned around, opened the door and stood on the threshold. Outside, he could see Joaquín, with the donkey and cart, surrounded by a crowd of amazed friends. His pretty Ana was standing among the girls at the well. For him, she was the loveliest of them all. Beatríz was sitting a few metres from him on the ground. She was playing with Manuel, telling him about the king, whom they were sure to see every day.

There was a better future for everyone in Madrid. Only not for Bartolomé. How was Juan going to make his wife understand

14

that, in the big city, cripples were mocked and abused – not just stared at, the way they were in the village, but spat on and humiliated by the indifferent masses. Behind his back, he could hear the despairing tears of the child.

'Take me with you, take me with you,' Bartolomé cried again and again.

Isabel tried in vain to comfort him.

In the end, Juan could bear it no longer. He turned around and said, 'If we take you with us, nobody must see you. You'll have to stay in our apartment, day in, day out.'

'Yes, Papa.'

'And if anyone comes to visit, you'll have to go into the back room.'

'Yes, Papa.' Bartolomé would promise anything, if only he could go with them to Madrid.

Juan tried once more to persuade his son. 'You'd be better off here in the village.'

But Bartolomé only shook his head silently. He didn't want to stay behind alone in the village. He belonged with his family. He was a Carrasco too.

Departure

VERY early next morning, they left the village. Isabel wondered if it was to be a parting for ever. She'd spent her whole life in this little place with its white houses and its stony fields and its olive and orange groves. How would her family get on in the big city?

Joaquín and Ana went ahead and led the donkey, which patiently pulled the heavily laden cart. Isabel and Juan followed behind the cart, Isabel with Manuel wrapped up in a bundle on her back, and Juan holding Beatríz by the hand. When the little girl got tired and cranky from all the walking, Juan lifted her up for a while on to the donkey's back. Bartolomé was being shaken from side to side as he sat on the cart, stuck in among the family's possessions: the bed, the table, the chairs, their household things and clothes.

They'd started out early in the morning, but now the hot sun was beating down on the little caravan. They planned to stop at the next inn, in the next village, for a rest and to let the noonday heat pass. Bartolomé stared longingly down the road, watching out for a church spire. His tongue felt like a leather cloth in his dry mouth. He didn't dare to ask for water. The water in the canteen was for the other children and for his mother, who had to walk. At last he spied, in the shimmering heat, the outline of a spire and several roofs.

'A village!' he called, stretching out his arm.

Joaquín and Ana hastened their steps. They could hardly wait to rest in the shade. Ana smacked the donkey impatiently on its sweat-drenched flank to hurry it up.

'Whoa!' called Juan suddenly from behind. The donkey stood stock still and the cart creaked to a halt. Ana and Joaquín turned around, wondering what was going on. Juan approached the cart and reached for the reins.

'Does anyone want a drink?' he asked.

They all shook their heads. The water in the leather water-bag was lukewarm by now and tasted brackish. Soon they'd get ice-cold fresh water from a deep village well.

Juan took a slug himself and wiped the drops of water from his chin with the back of his hand. Then he offered the water-bag to Bartolomé.

'Drink up,' he ordered him. 'Drink till you're no longer thirsty.'

Bartolomé did as he was told, though he didn't understand why he had to finish the stale-tasting water. Juan waited patiently. After Bartolomé had given him back the water-bag, Juan opened one of the chests. It was empty, except for one blanket.

'Climb in,' he commanded.

Bartolomé gave his father a horrified look. Was he supposed to crawl into this little chest?

'Go on!' said Juan curtly.

'Juan,' protested Isabel softly.

'From now on, he'll have to stick to the rule: he mustn't let any stranger see him. If he doesn't co-operate, then I can always send him back to Tomáz.'

17

With clenched teeth, Bartolomé crawled into the chest. The lid slammed over him. Daylight squeezed into the dark through cracks in the wood, but the heat was almost unbearable. Perspiration rolled off him in bucketfuls.

Bartolomé could feel the donkey starting to move again and the slow, wobbly forward movement of the cart over the uneven road surface. He tried to lie in such a way that his mouth was as near as possible to the biggest crack, so that he could breathe fresh air. The rough woollen blanket scratched his sweaty skin. But when his father had made a decision, he stuck to it.

The village was much like their home place. A few houses and a church around a dusty village square with a well. At the edge of the village was a little tavern. A farmer had set up a few tables in the shade of his olive trees. Here Juan stopped. He treated himself to a glass of wine. Isabel went with the children to the square to get water. Bartolomé stayed in his prison and listened to the conversation between his father and the owner of the little bar.

'I'm on my way to Madrid,' said Juan, 'together with my family.'

'If only I could do that!' said the tavern-keeper with a sigh. 'But my wife is afraid I would find no work there, and that she and our daughters would starve in the streets. Here we have a farm, and the bar brings in a bit of money. Only a fool would give that up, she says.'

'I have work,' said Juan proudly. 'I am coachman to the Infanta of Spain. I have taken an apartment in Madrid, and my sons will have a better future there. They'll learn a trade.'

Bartolomé's heart leapt. His father had plans for him, then. He was to learn a trade. If that was really possible, he'd go the whole way to Madrid in the chest without a word.

'Sons. We hoped for that. But it was not to be,' said the tavern-keeper sadly.

Juan nodded thoughtfully. He was glad he had been spared that fate.

'Both my sons will do well in Madrid, if they work hard. And I'll make sure they do!'

Both his sons?

But he has three sons, thought Bartolomé. Did he not count? Bartolomé pressed his fists to his ears. He didn't want to hear his father's voice any more.

Isabel came back with the children and the freshly filled water-bag.

'I drank so much water,' cried Beatríz, 'that my stomach is ice-cold and it's gurgling.'

Juan laughed. 'Then we'll eat,' he announced.

Isabel got the basket from the cart and shared out bread, hard-boiled eggs, cheese, tomatoes, olives and peppers. Once, when the bar-owner had gone into the house to pour Juan another mug of wine, Isabel snuck the lid of the chest open and pushed in a piece of bread.

'You'll get more once we're clear of the village,' she promised Bartolomé.

Let me out! Bartolomé wanted to yell. But he didn't do it. Instead, he stuffed the bread in big wodges into his mouth and chewed angrily. It tasted salty.

As the midday heat abated, they moved on. As soon as the cart was out of sight of the village, they stopped. Juan lifted Bartolomé out of the chest. He was dripping with sweat, and he had a heat rash on his legs, arms and face.

'I don't want to go back to the village,' said Bartolomé,

although Juan hadn't said a word about that.

Juan put him back in his place between the chests and the bed. The leftovers from lunch were waiting for him there, wrapped up in a cloth – another piece of bread, some cheese, olives, an egg and a few fresh figs.

'I didn't get any figs,' moaned Beatríz, watching from the donkey's back as Bartolomé was about to put one of the sweet fruits into his mouth.

'Those are Bartolomé's figs,' her father said sharply. He felt guilty that the midday rest had lasted so long.

Bartolomé hesitated. There were only a few fruits, and he could smell their sweet, heavy fragrance. He struggled with himself.

'Beatríz and Manuel can have them,' he said at last.

Juan nodded and took the figs. Bartolomé tried to see if there was an acknowledging look in his father's eyes, but he had turned away and was sticking a fig into Manuel's mouth.

He held the other two out to Beatríz. 'You can have them if you'll walk a bit now,' he said.

Beatríz pulled a face.

Maybe she'll refuse, and I'll get the figs back, Bartolomé hoped.

'He's allowed to sit the whole time,' whinged Beatríz. 'And he's much older than me.'

Juan lifted Beatríz down immediately from the donkey's back.

'You'll walk now,' he said, putting her down roughly on the stony road. He pressed the figs into her hand. 'You should be thankful that you have two strong, healthy legs, and that you aren't a cripple.'

The Mill

THE afternoon went on for ever. They were still on the road when dusk began to fall. Juan had miscalculated. He had expected to make better progress. Now he had to hold Beatríz steady on the donkey so that she wouldn't fall down from tiredness. He used the other hand to lead the animal.

Joaquín had fallen behind ages ago and was dragging along, exhausted, behind the others. Ana held on with one hand to the side of the cart and allowed herself to be pulled along, her eyes half-closed, rather than really walking herself. Isabel did not complain, but Manuel seemed to get heavier with every step.

'We can't sleep out of doors!'

'There's a mill at the next bridge. We'll spend the night there. It's not far.' Juan urged his family to get a move on. The only weapon he had was a dagger, and it was dangerous to travel after sunset without protection. Everyone had heard stories of vagabonds or robbers who wouldn't think twice about murdering travellers in order to get hold of their goods and chattels, no matter how little they were worth.

The first stars were already twinkling in the sky when at last they saw the grey silhouette of the mill on the horizon between a long row of pine trees, stretching up against the sky like black torches.

Joaquín, Ana and Isabel were too tired to be happy about it. They stumbled forward, too tired to think. Bartolomé, however, was wide awake. He had slept for a while after he'd eaten, and now he was sitting with his hump leaning against the bed, looking at the astonishing universe above his head.

If I were up there, he thought, *then I would be able to see everything: the village, the road, the mill between the pines, even Madrid, without being seen myself.*

When they reached a point where there was only the bridge between them and the mill, Juan bent over Bartolomé and opened the chest. Bartolomé took one last look at the mill. In spite of the dark sky, it seemed to him now to be more white than grey. Perhaps that was because the pines behind it were so black, or because the stars shone so brightly over it. With this image before his eyes, he allowed himself to be bundled into the chest.

Juan locked the lid carefully.

As if he's afraid I won't stay in here, thought Bartolomé angrily. In fact he would never disobey his father's orders. If his father could not love him as he loved Joaquín and Manuel, Bartolomé could at least get his attention by being obedient.

Juan led his family over the bridge, through a gate in the fence to the door of the mill, and knocked.

'You can't leave Bartolomé outside all by himself,' hissed Isabel.

'We'll take the chest in,' answered Juan curtly. He'd decided that, apart from in their own village, Bartolomé would have to remain hidden from strangers. A man stood by his decisions.

The miller opened the door cautiously, but when Juan explained what he wanted and said that he would pay cash for their lodgings and a pot of warm soup, he became more hospitable. He showed Juan the stable, where the donkey and cart would be safe.

Joaquín unloaded the sleeping mats and blankets, the chest and the little wooden box with Isabel's jewellery from the cart. The miller indicated a place where they could sleep in the grain loft. Joaquín and Ana had to carry the bedding and the jewellery box up, and Juan lifted the chest onto his back and, before the eyes of the curious miller family, he climbed carefully up the steep ladder with his burden.

They'll think I keep gold and silver in it, Juan thought, setting the chest down beside the millstone. In the meantime, Isabel had made a sleeping place with the mats and blankets.

'You'll stay in the chest till we're all up,' Juan warned Bartolomé, without opening the lid. Then he went downstairs to eat the soup that the miller's wife had hurriedly stretched with water and bulked out with eggs and tomatoes.

Beatríz was too tired to spoon up the hot liquid. Isabel ladled a little of it into her and then carried her up the narrow ladder.

Before her head had touched the pillow, Bartolomé could hear her soft, even breathing. He waited patiently. A little later, Ana and Joaquín came. Joaquín knocked on the chest.

'It was a thick vegetable soup with eggs,' he announced through the lid. 'Pity you won't get any. But you can't be hungry anyway. You didn't have to bestir yourself today.'

Joaquín's feet hurt. Having pulled off his patched boots, he could see that they were swollen and fiery red. Why should Bartolomé get soup, when he'd ridden on the cart all day?

Ana rebuked him: 'He can't help it. He's a cripple and he can't walk like us.'

But she was too exhausted to make Joaquín apologise to Bartolomé. Tears sprang to her eyes when she took off her shoes and found big blisters on her heels and toes. She couldn't imagine how she'd be able to walk the next day. She crept under her blanket without saying anything more.

'I'm sorry,' muttered Joaquín, lying down beside her.

Bartolomé wasn't allowed out of his prison until his parents came up to the loft, carrying the peacefully sleeping Manuel. Then he found himself a place between his sleeping brothers and sisters.

'Are you still hungry?' asked Isabel in a tired whisper. Bartolomé shook his head.

In the morning, they were awoken by the grinding and grating sounds of beams, wheels and millstones. The miller had opened the millrace outside and the great millwheel was starting to creak and turn. He'd be up the ladder any minute now to grind the corn and fill it into sacks.

Isabel shook the tired children awake and started to roll up the bedding. Juan gave Bartolomé a silent look and nodded towards the chest. Bartolomé knew what that meant. He crept over quickly and climbed into the chest. Juan shut the lid tightly.

Torre de la Parada

THE second day of the journey was much the same as the first, only that every step was more difficult. Joaquín and Ana didn't want to go ahead and lead the donkey. Instead, they walked behind the cart, and when Juan wasn't looking, they hung on to it so that they could get a bit of a pull.

After the first hour of marching, Beatríz moaned so much that Juan finally gave in and let her ride on the cart. Bartolomé spent most of the time in the chest, because the road went through one village and hamlet after another, and they were so close together that Juan decided it was a waste of time to keep stopping the cart for the short times in between villages.

'When we reach the forest, he can come out,' Juan said to Isabel. She didn't protest.

On this day, Juan made the family continue with their journey after only a short lunch break. Looking into Ana's tired eyes, he comforted her: 'We'll be at the forest soon. It's cool and shady there.'

Ana shrugged her shoulders. She couldn't care less any more that the sun was burning, that she was thirsty even though she could drink as much as she wanted, that her feet were blistered and that her legs hurt.

Juan tried to encourage his children: 'In the middle of this wood is Torre de la Parada, the king's hunting lodge. We'll lodge there for the night.'

Ana nodded without interest. She couldn't work up any enthusiasm for this castle as long as it was far away, out of sight. Beatríz cheered up, however. She'd had a good rest. She looked at her father with big eyes.

'Does the king live there?' she asked.

Juan said that he didn't. 'If he were there, we wouldn't be allowed to sleep there,' he said.

'Are we going to sneak in secretly?' Joaquín's eyes were bright with excitement. He'd forgotten how tired he was.

Juan frowned crossly. He wasn't a vagabond.

'The royal master of the hunt, Don Pacheco, has given me permission to stable the donkey and cart and to spend the night in the castle.'

The king, his castle, a hunt master, thought Isabel. She hadn't realised that Juan had such a high position in court and that he knew such important people personally. She gave him a thoughtful look, which pleased Juan.

'Can't we go on?' said Beatríz impatiently.

Ana sighed. 'You don't have to walk,' she said sharply. 'You're getting a lift.'

Juan laughed. But when he saw that Ana had tears in her eyes, he lifted Beatríz down from the cart.

'You rode the whole morning. Now you can walk for a bit, and Ana can ride,' he decided, taking no notice of Beatríz's protestations. He took her by the hand and they walked on. Ana climbed up quickly on to the cart.

They reached the forest late in the afternoon. Juan stopped the cart in the shade and Bartolomé was finally able to get out of the chest. He was amazed. He would never have thought that so many trees could grow in one spot. 'They'd take the sight from your eyes,' he murmured in surprise. Even the road, which yesterday had wound like a long white ribbon up hill and down dale, disappeared here between the tree trunks.

Ana and Beatríz swapped places again, and even Joaquín seemed to find new strength. He and Ana led the donkey together.

'When will we get to the castle?' he asked.

'Soon,' answered Juan.

'What does it look like?' Now Ana was asking questions too. 'Is it very big? Are there many servants there?'

'Torre de la Parada is only a little hunting lodge, and the king is hardly ever there. But there's a big staff all the same. They take care of the building, the garden and the game park. For this reason, Bartolomé will have to sleep in the chest tonight, in the stable.'

'But ...' Isabel started to say.

'Nothing will happen to him,' Juan interrupted her. 'But I can't bring a locked chest into the castle in full sight of Don Pacheco. It would look as if I had something to hide from him.'

Isabel said nothing, though she didn't think it was right to let Bartolomé spend a whole night alone in a strange place.

But it was Juan who had made these decisions, and it wasn't her place to criticise him.

As Joaquín led the donkey around the next bend in the road, he came upon a long low stone wall.

'Does this wall belong to the castle?' he asked curiously.

'Yes. The park is behind it,' explained Juan. 'We'll come to the entrance shortly.'

27

And sure enough, after a few hundred metres, a white gravel road led off the main road to a gate in the wall. A small house stood near it, surrounded by juniper bushes. An old man was dozing on a bench in front of the house.

'Carlos the gatekeeper,' said Juan, lowering his voice. Bartolomé knew what that meant. He crept obediently into his chest. But he protested all the more loudly inside his head. Beatríz, Ana and Joaquín would see the castle and would even sleep there, whereas he wouldn't be allowed so much as a glimpse of it.

If he'd only praise me for my obedience, thought Bartolomé bitterly. But Juan seemed to take it for granted.

Bartolomé tried to peep through the cracks in the chest, but all he could see was the bedstead and the basket of provisions for the journey.

Juan greeted the gatekeeper confidently and led his family up the long avenue to the hall door. The castle was not large. It was really just a stout square tower, with a two-storey building stuck on to it. The two-storey building had a red façade with white stone inlay. For Ana, Beatríz and Joaquín, it was the biggest building they had ever seen.

'That tower,' gasped Ana. 'It's so high, I can't imagine how it was built.'

Juan beamed. 'Wait till you get to Madrid. In comparison with the Cathedral of San Isidor, this tower is hardly worth talking about.'

Ana looked disbelievingly at him. He had to be joking.

A footman came walking towards the little band. Beatríz tried to hide between the chests on the cart; Ana, Joaquín and Isabel stood bashfully behind Juan. He tried to hide his own uncertainty. Don Pacheco had indeed offered him accommodation for the night, but the higher the position a person held, the less were his friendship and favour to be relied upon. Juan had driven the little Infanta Margarita to the hunting lodge in the spring of the previous year. At that time, he'd spent the night in the stable. There had been a shortage of space, as the king had had a big party to stay. The numerous noblemen and ladies had brought their valets and maids, footmen and coachmen, and the quarters usually occupied by the king's staff were so full that Juan preferred to make his bed in the soft straw.

He hadn't had a quiet night. Marquis, the king's favourite white steed, had had a bout of colic, and Juan had spent hours walking the feverish horse, who was tormented by terrible pains, up and down the yard, wiping the sweat off his coat and speaking softly to him. The colic finally abated in the early hours of the morning. The horse's life had been saved.

Don Pacheco, who was also responsible for stabling the horses, had embraced Juan gratefully. What the king would have done if his fine mount had died didn't bear thinking of. Since that day, there'd been a kind of friendship between Juan and the supervisor of the hunting lodge in spite of the difference in status between them. Every time Don Pacheco had business in Alcázar, the royal residence in Madrid, he made a point of looking in on the coachman and, if they had time, inviting him to have a glass of wine with him. On the few occasions that Juan was required to drive the Infanta to Torre de la Parada, he was allowed to take a rest in Don Pacheco's apartment, while a footman saw to the coach and horses. But Juan couldn't be sure he could rely on this friendship.

The footman who was approaching them now recognised Juan and gave a slight bow. 'Don Pacheco is expecting you, Don Carrasco,' he announced politely.

Juan nodded, relieved. The footman rustled up a stable hand, and Juan put the donkey's bridle into his hand.

'Won't we need our mats and blankets for the night?' hissed Isabel.

Juan shook his head. What would Don Pacheco think if his hospitable invitation to spend the night with him was undermined like that?

The stable hand took the donkey and cart away. Inside his chest, Bartolomé could hear the lad taking the reins off the donkey and leading him to the trough. The hurried, hungry chewing of the animal reached Bartolomé's ears in his hiding place. He wished he could climb out of his narrow chest, but he had to wait till he could be sure that there was no one in the stable except the animals. It took for ever. At last, he heard the heavy stable door banging shut and being bolted.

Now Bartolomé raised the lid and crept out. It was pitch dark in the stable. All around him he could hear the soft sounds of many animals, standing quietly in the straw, munching. He could feel the warmth of their bodies.

He felt around for the basket. He pulled a big chunk of bread hungrily from the loaf. He found a few hard-boiled eggs and dried tomatoes. He sat on the bedstead and began to eat. He didn't care that he'd eaten more than his father would normally allow him, the cripple. After all, the others were dining in the castle of the king. In Bartolomé's imagination, they were sitting at a large, beautifully laid table, brightly lit by candles in heavy silver candelabra. Waiters were carrying solid gold platters on which enormous pieces of meat and pies steamed. Also bowls filled with all kinds of delicacies were being offered to them by lackeys. His parents and brothers and sisters were sitting there like princes and princesses, stuffing themselves.

Bartolomé laughed softly. The image in his head was so vivid, he could even hear Joaquín giving politely suppressed burps, and he could see Beatríz rolling off her chair with a bulging tummy. If they had tummy-ache in the morning after their fancy meal, he would have no sympathy for them.

Arrival

NOBODY had tummy-ache in the morning. The opposite, in fact. Don Pacheco had drunk a glass of wine with Juan, but otherwise he seemed to assume that his guests had already eaten. They had spent a cold, draughty night on the stone floor of the unused kitchen quarters of the hunting lodge, without their mats and blankets.

'There was no breakfast either,' Joaquín complained, as they hurried down the drive of the castle. Bartolomé smiled in his chest, up on the cart. It had been warm in the stable, and he'd had no shortage of food. He remembered Father Rodriquez, the old priest in their village. One evening, when Bartolomé had been sitting on the stone steps watching the other children playing, the priest had picked him up, carried him into the church and shown him the great wooden cross hanging on the wall above the high altar.

'The last shall be first,' the priest had said, pointing at the cross. Bartolomé hadn't believed it at the time. He was the last in the village, and he could not imagine that ever changing. *Until last night*, thought Bartolomé, pleased to hear Joaquín impatiently asking his father when on earth they could stop and have some breakfast. Last night, he'd been the first. It was a lovely feeling and it might even be a sign. Maybe an even bigger miracle would take place in Madrid that would turn him, the cripple, into a proper son.

But whatever miracles might happen in Madrid, Bartolomé had to get back into his prison long before they got to the city gate. As the narrow road emerged from the forest, it met a broad road. Countless coaches and riders passed them in the next few hours. All important people, together with their noble wives and children and their servants, all apparently wanting to get away from Madrid, to escape the hot, muggy city even if only for a day.

On the roadside, it seemed that every peasant who had a table and a couple of benches had set them out in the shade of a tree. In these temporary little bars, the peasants sold wine and little portions of food to hungry travellers. Merchants with carts and hand-baskets offered all kinds of wares: vegetables, fruit, baked goods and sweets. Their loud voices boomed through the air.

Bartolomé heard Beatríz whining in the midday heat. She wanted to take a little rest and have something to eat and drink. But Juan went plodding on, past all these temptations. He wanted to reach Madrid before dusk.

As Juan led his wife and children through the western gate into the city, they clung anxiously to the side of the cart. They had never seen so many houses and people in one spot. Nearly every building had several storeys. Some façades were beautifully decorated and there were windows of glass in which the rays of the sun sparkled. The streets through which they went were paved with great flat stones over which the cart rolled easily.

'Calle Zaragoza, behind Plaza Major. That's where we live. In case we get split up, that's where you are to go,' Juan warned them. 'Ask somebody the way.'

He sat Beatríz on the back of the donkey. Ana and Joaquín gave him a horrified look. They would never be able to find their way in this enormous city.

Juan took no notice of their terror. He marched on, set on reaching his goal, pulling the donkey by the bridle behind him. Ana and Joaquín took each other by the hand. With his other hand, Joaquín held tightly to the cart. Even Isabel was gripped by fear as they left the broad streets and stepped into the narrow alleyways between high houses. Here, where it was so narrow, the people seemed to crowd in. Isabel believed she'd never seen so many people at once. She'd like to have walked with Juan, taking his arm. But that wasn't the way it happened. Keeping her eyes fixed on Joaquín and Ana's backs, she hurried along behind them.

Manuel was bound securely on her back. He'd slept soundly for most of the journey. Now, however, he was woken by the noise of the city. He didn't know which way to look. There was so much to see.

They came to a marketplace full of pens with live animals for sale. Manuel pulled excitedly at Isabel's headscarf when he noticed the hens, geese, goats and sheep. He wanted her to stop. But Isabel had eyes only for the cart and her children. She didn't want to lose sight of them.

Juan turned out of the marketplace into a wide street that led to the Cathedral of San Isidor. When they reached the square in front of it, he stopped to wipe the perspiration from his forehead. They were nearly there.

Ana, Beatríz, Joaquín and Isabel stared open-mouthed at the imposing towers that seemed to reach as high as the clouds. But it was Manuel who noticed something familiar in all this unimaginable splendour. 'Barmo, Barmo!' he shouted, pointing excitedly at the cathedral.

Barmo? Isabel swung around towards the cart. That's what Manuel called Bartolomé. Surely he couldn't have disobeyed his father's order and crept out of the chest? No, the chest was tightly closed.

'Barmo, Barmo!' Manuel kept calling. He was so excited that he tried to wriggle out of the cloth that bound him to his mother's back.

Isabel looked where Manuel was pointing and was horrified. There, in a niche in the grey façade sat Bartolomé, miserable and in rags. It was only when she looked again that she realised that it was not her own son but another crippled child, stretching out his hand to the passersby, who took no notice of him.

Shocked, Isabel looked away. Tramps had come into the village from time to time, homeless old men and women, childless or abandoned by their children. People gave them a crust of bread, sometimes a bowl of soup. But she'd never seen such a pitiable little child begging. Did he not have any parents?

Juan had also noticed the little creature. 'Now you know why I didn't want to bring him,' he said in a hard voice. Without waiting for Isabel's answer, he gripped the bridle more tightly and walked on. The little caravan set off again slowly, following him. Isabel did not look back as they left the cathedral square.

New Home

CALLE ZARAGOZA was a narrow, densely inhabited alleyway near the Alcázar and the great Cathedral of San Isidor. Juan stopped the cart in front of one of the buildings and opened the door. A dark hallway stretched out in front of him. Noises came crowding out of the house, the crying of a child, shrill girls' voices and the clucking of hens. It smelt of food and of drains.

'This is our new home,' said Juan.

'Do we have to live with strangers?' hissed Ana, disappointed. She had dreamt of a roomy house with a garden.

'In Madrid, only the rich people have their own houses,' explained Juan shortly. He looked at Isabel. 'We have the whole first floor all to ourselves,' he said, trying to set her mind at rest. 'We have a big room at the front, facing the street, and a small room at the back, looking out onto the yard. Upstairs lives Señora Lopez, the widow of an apothecary. She owns the house. Don Zorilla and his wife rent the ground floor. He's a royal chamberlain, and he has three daughters, Jeronima, Luzia and Augustina. Jeronima is a little simple, but she's a good soul. You don't need to be afraid of her. But at the same time, you shouldn't annoy her.' Juan looked sternly at Joaquín.

'Don Zorilla found the apartment for me. I owe him a favour because of that. It's not easy to find a reasonable place in

Madrid in a good area. Señora Lopez gave me a good deal on the rent, and in return you'll do her washing, Isabel, and Ana will look after her children from time to time.'

Everyone helped with the unpacking, except Manuel and Bartolomé, who wasn't allowed out of the chest yet. Juan had to take the donkey and cart back before evening. Quickly, they put the chests, the bedstead, the chairs and the rest of the luggage in the hall.

Juan gave Isabel a big key. 'For the door to the apartment,' he explained. At home in the village, they'd had no key, just a bolt that Isabel used to fasten the door at night.

'I'll carry the big pieces up when I get home,' said Juan.

'May I come with you?' asked Joaquín. Juan thought it over. Joaquín should really be helping the others to carry up the chests. On the other hand, it would be good to familiarise him a bit with the area, so that he could show Isabel the way to the well and the market the following morning. Juan nodded.

The pair of them disappeared. Isabel watched them go with a worried look in her eyes. She was a little afraid of having to go into the strange apartment on her own.

'Can we go up?' asked Ana. She was curious and wanted to see the rooms.

'It's so dark here, Mama,' complained Beatríz.

Isabel screwed up her courage. 'Beatríz will take the jewellery box and she'll hold Manuel's hand. Ana and I will carry up the chest with Bartolomé in it.'

'Can he not get out down here?' asked Ana.

Isabel shook her head. 'No, we're not the only people in the house, and nobody can be allowed to see him.'

Ana said nothing. So far, none of the other occupants of the house had observed their arrival. Why would they suddenly put in an appearance, all agog?

The stairs were narrow and steep and even darker than the hall. They kept banging the chest against the wall. When they got to the landing, Isabel and Ana put it down. In the dusk, Isabel could make out a brown wooden door. That must be the door to their apartment. Isabel felt for the lock, and opened up. Light streamed onto the landing. The room was bright and spacious with two windows. Apart from a large clay pot, it was empty.

Isabel pushed the chest in and opened the lid. Bartolomé crept out. The sudden light blinded him. He held his hands up to his face and tried to stretch his cramped and crooked body.

Beatríz and Ana went barging around the room. Ana had opened the second door on the far wall. There was a poky little room in there, with a window high on the wall. This room was also empty.

Isabel looked around, working out where she would put the various pieces of furniture. The bed would have to go in the big room. The children could sleep in the back room on their mats, and she could put three or four of the chests in there too. The front room would also be their living room during the day. The chairs would go by the windows. That way, she and Ana could do their sewing in good light. They might even be able to make lace to sell. Isabel had picked up, reading between the lines of what Juan had said, that the rent was still too dear and that they could use every extra penny they could make. The table fitted in by the bed, which could also be used as a seat in the daytime. She'd put the stools on the other side of the table.

'Mama,' Ana interrupted her thoughts. 'Where are we going to cook?' She hadn't seen a fireplace in either of the rooms.

Isabel grinned and pointed to the round-bellied clay pot. 'We'll cook on that. It's a clay oven. You feed it coal or wood, and you can heat a pot or a frying pan on top of it.'

Bartolomé had hauled himself up out of the chest by now. He couldn't cross the room on his own, without any furniture to hang on to. He stumbled along by the wall until he reached one of the two windows. He wanted to see Madrid at last with his own eyes. But the window was too high. Beatríz stood next to him on her tippy toes. Bartolomé tried to imitate her, but in vain. With his club feet and mangled toes, he couldn't manage it.

Suddenly he was lifted up.

'Now you can look out,' said Ana kindly.

Bartolomé looked delightedly down at the street. At last he could make sense of all the sounds he'd been hearing. All the people with wildly differing voices thronging the streets. The sound of cartwheels and the clip-clop of hooves. Patiently, Ana held him tight. Bartolomé kept making new discoveries. Washing hanging on lines that were strung out across the street. A lady with a fancy hairdo, followed by her servants, who were laden down with shopping baskets. A knife sharpener with his handcart. A musician with a flute and – Bartolomé's eyes grew wide with astonishment – a comical creature sitting on his shoulder, dressed like a little man in red trousers, a white shirt, a green waistcoat and a black hat. It had a hairy face and around its neck it wore a collar with a chain, the other end of which was fastened to the broad belt of the musician. The animal – or was it really a tiny dwarf? – was twirling the flute-player's hair with nimble fingers. A mob of children and adults had gathered around him. When the creature turned around, Bartolomé could see that his trousers had a hole in them, out of which snaked a long tail.

'What is that?' cried Bartolomé.

'I don't know.' Ana had never seen such an extraordinary thing either.

Isabel came to the window with Manuel in her arms.

'It's a monkey,' she said. 'An animal from Africa. They are like humans, only much smaller and very hairy.'

'Get away from the window at once!' Juan's voice thundered angrily through the room. They had not heard him and Joaquín coming.

Ana let Bartolomé drop quickly. Manuel began to cry with the shock. Beatríz's lips started to quiver. What had they done wrong? They'd only looked out of the window.

Juan banged the door of the apartment shut. '*Anyone* could have seen him!'

They all knew who he meant.

'It won't happen again,' Isabel promised hastily.

'Certainly it won't. From now on, Bartolomé can only be in the front room in the evenings, when the door has been barred for the night and the shutters are closed.'

Thus his father banished him to the back bedroom. His head hanging, Bartolomé allowed Ana to take him there. As the door closed over, he leant his head against the cool stone wall. He suddenly had a headache, and his throat was burning. The room with its little window, too high up in the wall to be reached, was just as much a prison as the chest had been. Nobody could see him here. Bartolomé started to cry quietly.

El Primo

BARTOLOMÉ'S days were all the same. He sat huddled alone in the little room for hours on end. In the evenings, when he was allowed to sit at the table in the big room, he listened enviously to the exciting stories of his brothers and sisters.

Juan went to work in the mornings and often he didn't come home until late in the evenings. He rarely had a day off. When he did, he would go walking sometimes with Manuel, Ana and Beatríz or he'd go shopping with their mother. Once he invited Joaquín for a glass of wine in a tavern. But mostly he went to bed and slept.

He hardly ever gave a thought to his dwarf son in the back room. If it made Isabel happy to have the child with her, it was fine by him, as long as Bartolomé stuck to the rules.

Juan had found an apprenticeship with a baker for Joaquín. 'People always need bread,' he said happily.

If Joaquín did well during his probationary period, then he'd get a proper apprenticeship contract and he would move in with the baker. For now, he had to leave the house every day long before dawn and he came home early in the afternoon, stumbling with exhaustion. Bits of dough would be clinging to his black hair, and his hands would be chapped from the dry flour.

'He'll get used to it,' Juan said, and he was right. After a while, the exhaustion disappeared and Joaquín was able to use his free afternoons to explore the city.

Ana, when she wasn't helping out around the house or sitting sewing by the window, spent many hours upstairs with the children of Señora Lopez, the apothecary's widow, so that lady could supervise her late husband's business, in which she still owned a share.

Señora Lopez was constantly in fear of being thrown out on her ear. Her eldest daughter Maria was only ten years old. Since her father's death the previous winter she had been betrothed to the new master apothecary. In a few years, after the wedding, or better still, after the birth of a grandson, Señora Lopez would finally be able to trust that her connection with the family of the apothecary would protect her from being swindled. Until then, she went to the shop several times a week to check the takings and the outgoings. That was when Ana took care of the youngest children, three-year-old Teresa and two-year-old Gaspar.

Maria often had to go with her mother. The apothecary, an older man – he was forty – was proud of his young fiancée and was pleased when she sat meekly in a corner beside him.

Beatríz had made friends with Augustina, the youngest daughter of Don Zorilla, the royal chamberlain. The two little girls played for hours in the back yard where there was a shed in which Señora Lopez's pig and hens were kept, and where there was also a latrine.

Manuel was a favourite with Doña Rosita, Don Zorilla's wife, who had no son of her own. Whenever Isabel scolded Manuel or wouldn't let him have his way or just didn't have time for him, he would scarper as soon as the door of the apartment was opened. He wasn't afraid of the steep stairs or the dark landing.

He banged his little fists on the door of the apartment downstairs. Doña Rosita always welcomed him with open arms and spoilt him with tasty morsels and attention. Isabel didn't like that.

On the other hand, she could get on with her work when Manuel was out of the way. She could well use the money she got for the lace she made, which she sold to a dressmaker. Life in Madrid was expensive. In the village, the children had gathered firewood without giving it a second thought, but here every log had to be paid for. The same with fruit and vegetables. They used to grow these themselves, but now they had to buy them at the market.

The whole family's days were filled with work and play. Except for Bartolomé. He missed the village. Locked into the little room, he thought longingly of the dusty village square, the white houses and the little church with its stone steps and the weather-beaten wooden porch from where he had watched the doings of the village.

Sometimes, when Isabel and Ana were alone, he was allowed into the big room in the daytime. He would sit quietly in a corner and watch them doing housework. But it never occurred to Isabel to give him a task to do. The sound of the street came pouring in through the big open windows of the apartment. Bartolomé listened longingly with his eyes closed and tried to imagine that he was taking part in the goings-on outside. But the more monotonous days that went by, the less he was able to conjure up this daydream and the quieter and sadder he got.

One afternoon, just as Bartolomé was quietly going mad in the little room, where he knew every chink in the wall and every crack in the floorboards, Joaquín came bursting in. He hunkered down on the floor opposite Bartolomé. His cheeks were red from running, and his eyes were blazing with excitement.

'Listen, Bartolomé!'

Bartolomé looked dully at Joaquín. He used to enjoy it when Joaquín told him about the wonderful things that went on in the city. He used to imagine that he had experienced it all himself. He had run behind coaches, had seen someone thieving in the marketplace and had gone walking along by the mighty walls of the royal palace of Alcázar. But those dreams had long lost their magic. Instead, Bartolomé felt more and more keenly how empty and lonely his own life was. He turned his head away, but Joaquín was not to be put off.

'I saw an important man,' he whispered.

Bartolomé sighed to himself. Joaquín's stories were always about important gentlemen and rich ladies.

'He was being carried in a sedan chair. I followed him. At San Isidor's Cathedral, he got out and …' Joaquín hesitated pointedly.

'And …?' asked Bartolomé without a great deal of interest in hearing the rest of the story.

'He was almost as small as you. But grown up. He had a beard and he wore an elegant suit of gleaming black damask.'

'A dwarf like me?'

'Yes, but rich and respectable. I asked one of the bearers about him. The dwarf is called Don Diego de Acedo. But they call him El Primo. He is a secretary in the royal court.'

'A secretary at court,' repeated Bartolomé.

Joaquín nodded. 'He writes letters and documents for the king. He lives in the palace and I bet he's well paid for his work, because he can afford his own sedan and bearers. Bartolomé, if only you could do that!'

Bartolomé bit his lip. A dwarf like him could have a job and he could allow himself to be seen, without anyone looking down on him. How come his father had kept this from him and had locked him up ·like an animal when in Madrid dwarves could work for the king?

'As a secretary, you would have influence at court. You could make sure I became court baker, and Ana and Beatríz could be lady's maids to the little Infanta.' Joaquín was weaving wonderful fantasies.

'I can't read and write,' Bartolomé interrupted him. 'I can't do anything except sit and look.'

Joaquín's mood changed, but only for a moment. 'You'll just have to learn,' he said. 'There must be schools in Madrid.'

Bartolomé gave a bitter laugh. 'I'm not even allowed to sit in the big room during the daytime. And you think that Papa would send me to school?'

Joaquín paced up and down. It irritated him that his fine plans were being destroyed by harsh reality. There had to be a way that Bartolomé could learn to read and write. Joaquín wondered if he could ask his father to send him to school in the afternoons. Then he could secretly pass on his knowledge to Bartolomé. On the other hand, he really didn't feel like spending his time at school after working hard. And anyway, a school like that would cost a lot. Definitely more than his father could afford.

But Bartolomé had been infected by Joaquín's plan.

'Maybe Ana could go to school in my place?'

'Papa definitely wouldn't pay to educate a girl,' Joaquín replied.

Bartolomé hung his head in disappointment. His crooked shoulders crumpled. He tried not to cry in front of Joaquín. A sob escaped him all the same.

Joaquín paused and looked down at him. Up to now, he'd been thinking more about himself than about his poor crippled brother. He began to realise what it must be like for him in the little room and that his plan meant much more to Bartolomé than to himself. He gave him a quick hug.

'Bartolomé, I promise you that you will learn to read and write,' he whispered.

Don Cristobal

FOR the next few days, Bartolomé was bursting with impatience. He could hardly wait to see Joaquín. In the afternoons, he sat in the little back bedroom. He listened intently, his ear to the door, to hear the quick footsteps of his brother on the stairs. Joaquín was aware how much faith Bartolomé was putting in him and decided to let Ana in on the plan. Maybe she would be able to think of a way to find a teacher for Bartolomé.

'But Papa mustn't get wind of it,' he warned her.

Ana nodded. 'He won't allow it,' she said, 'because nobody is allowed to see Bartolomé.'

'And I can't think either where we are going to get the money to pay for lessons,' declared Joaquín.

'If we let Mama in on the plan, she'd be able to help by saving on the housekeeping,' Ana said. She had noticed that Isabel was worried about Bartolomé, because he had got so quiet and sad. Now his eyes were shining again.

'We won't tell her until I have found a teacher,' Joaquín decided. 'She might forbid us, on account of Papa.'

Joaquín's search ran into a blind alley almost immediately. Anyone who was able to read and write had no time for teaching, or demanded a lot of money to teach this fine art.

When Joaquín noticed one day that Bartolomé's eyes had dulled again, he made his mind up. After work, he went to the

Franciscan monastery and knocked. An old monk, bare-footed and wearing a simple brown habit, opened the gate. Joaquín excused himself shyly. He couldn't think how to put his request into words.

'My son, what can I do for you?' asked the monk kindly.

'My name is Joaquín Carrasco, and I have a request,' said Joaquín bashfully.

'Of God or of me, Joaquín?'

'Of you, Father.'

The monk nodded and waited patiently. He seemed to have all the time in the world.

'My brother, Bartolomé ... he needs to learn to read and write,' Joaquín stammered.

'This isn't a school, Joaquín.'

'I know. But my father would never send him to school.'

'Your father probably has other plans for your brother. As a son, you should not question your father's decisions.'

Joaquín looked into the monk's kindly face. 'I know, Father, but ...' He was ashamed to say what he had to say. He had never before said a bad word about his father. 'Forgive me, Father, but my father locks Bartolomé in a back bedroom. Bartolomé sits there like a prisoner, and no outsider is allowed to see him.'

Don Cristobal, for that was the old monk's name, saw before him a skinny, lanky lad who was revealing a family secret, his face ablaze. Even if he didn't hear confessions himself, he knew that behind many a closed door in Madrid things happened that would horrify an old man like him, and would make him doubt God's goodness. And now it was his turn to search for the right words.

'Would you like me to speak to your father?' he offered finally. 'Sometimes a conversation can change things.' *Or not*, he added to himself.

Joaquín shook his head in horror. 'He mustn't find out that I've been here.'

'Is it that bad? Does he mistreat your brother?'

'No, he would never do a thing like that,' said Joaquín quickly. 'He's ashamed of him, I think. He is so ashamed that nobody is allowed to see Bartolomé. Bartolomé hasn't grown. His body is crooked. He has club feet and he can hardly walk on them.'

'A dwarf,' murmured Don Cristobal.

Joaquín nodded. 'A dwarf, a cripple, a freak – that's what an outsider would call him. But he is my brother and he is clever and he learns quickly.'

Joaquín's cheeks were glowing, not with shame now but with enthusiasm.

'If he can learn to read and write, then he can become the king's secretary, like El Primo. He is respected by everyone and doesn't have to hide away.'

'El Primo,' said Don Cristobal. 'Joaquín, you must know that there are hundreds of dwarves and cripples who eke out a living as miserable beggars on the streets of Madrid, and also probably many like your brother who are hidden from the mockery of the world in dark rooms and hovels. El Primo's story is most unusual. God's grace has rested on him in a very special way.'

'What El Primo has achieved, Bartolomé could do too.'

'Of course. God's grace could rest on your poor brother in a special way also. But who are we mere humans to know where and how God's grace will fall?' answered Don Cristobal mildly.

'Father, he must learn to read and write. Please help him. I promised him, and I can pay. Not much, but you won't have to teach him for nothing.'

Joaquín gave the old monk a beseeching look.

'You want me to go to your house, behind your father's back, and teach your brother to read and write? Have you any idea what you are asking?'

Don Cristobal shook his head. He could never do such a thing. The abbot wouldn't allow it, and without his permission he couldn't leave the monastery. If the child could come to him, though …

Joaquín seemed to read Don Cristobal's thoughts.

'Father, if he could come to you, would you teach him?' he asked.

'I have a lot to do. I am not just the porter here,' murmured Don Cristobal. 'I have to look after the church and the garden too.'

'While you are teaching Bartolomé, I could work in the garden,' Joaquín offered. He had a feeling that the monk was almost ready to help. He had no idea how he could get Bartolomé to the monastery. He'd have to get his head around that later.

'And I'll pay you too,' he went on.

'I can't take money,' said Don Cristobal. As a monk, he could call nothing his own apart from his habit.

'Or I could use the money to buy …'

'Candles?' Don Cristobal suggested.

Joaquín's heart leapt. Was the monk trying to say that he would teach Bartolomé?

'A candle for Our Lady,' Don Cristobal decided.

Joaquín was jubilant. Forgetting that the monk was a holy man, he hugged him hard.

Don Cristobal gave in.

'Twice a week, Tuesdays and Saturdays, for an hour at

lunchtime.' Don Cristobal added, 'But only if your father allows it.'

Joaquín nodded. It was all fine with him. The monk would teach Bartolomé. That was all that mattered.

As Don Cristobal closed the gate behind Joaquín, he decided he would wait until the first lesson before asking the abbot for permission.

The Secret Plan

'WE have to do it!'

Bartolomé had never seen his brother so determined. As confident as his father, bossy even, Joaquín was speaking to Isabel.

'We can't tell him. Not yet anyway. He would forbid it,' Joaquín insisted.

Bartolomé looked at his mother. Would she agree to keep the secret from his father?

Isabel felt she was being steamrolled into it. Joaquín, Ana and Bartolomé were all lined up in front of her. She tried to withstand the pleading looks of her children. She couldn't allow such a thing. Juan was her husband. She must not keep anything from him.

'Mama.' Ana came right up to Isabel. 'Mama, if Bartolomé can read and write, then he has a future.'

'He can earn his own money that way,' Joaquín added.

'Then maybe Papa will be proud of me,' Bartolomé whispered.

Isabel had to look into his great, dark eyes. She could sense his longing. It would be wonderful if Bartolomé learnt a profession.

But Juan would be terribly angry at the deception. No, she could not allow it.

'Nobody must see him. Your father has forbidden it,' she said quietly.

'I know,' said Joaquín. 'That's why I am going to transport

him in the laundry basket. Ana will come too and people will think I am helping her with the washing.'

'We've had a trial run. Bartolomé fits, and Joaquín is strong enough to lift up the basket and to carry it. We'll show you!'

Ana's face glowed with enthusiasm. Without waiting for an answer, she led her dwarf brother to the basket and heaved him in. Bartolomé made himself as small as possible. His black mop of hair disappeared beneath the rim of the basket. Ana put a few bits of washing on top of him.

'While Bartolomé is studying, I'll wash a few clothes, and everyone will see us coming home with the wet laundry. Nobody will have a clue what is going on,' Ana assured her mother. 'There will be no questions asked.'

Joaquín knelt in front of the laundry basket, slipped his arms into the straps and stood up, wobbling. Drops of sweat beaded his forehead as he walked up and down the room taking little steps.

'How far is it to the monastery?' Isabel asked in spite of herself.

'Not far,' gasped Joaquín. 'I can do it.'

Isabel hesitated. She had never seen her children so set on anything, and if they carried Bartolomé through the streets like this, they would not be breaking Juan's edict.

No, that's not right, thought Isabel. The monk would see Bartolomé. But did a monk count anyway? Was he not pledged to silence? This thought eased Isabel's conscience.

'Mama?' Bartolomé stuck his head over the edge of the basket, like a cuckoo breaking out of the egg. Isabel couldn't help but laugh.

'Can I?' asked Bartolomé.

Isabel nodded. She couldn't help herself. Bartolomé's joy was so great that he would have leapt out of the basket and jumped right into his mother's arms, if only he had been capable of it.

HIS knees wobbling from the effort, Joaquín reached the monastery gate. Nobody in the busy streets had taken any notice of them. Nobody could have guessed that the two excited children were hiding a secret in their laundry basket.

Joaquín knocked at the gate, which Don Cristobal immediately opened. He had been waiting for them.

'Where is he?' he asked in surprise when he could see no crippled dwarf.

'In the basket,' answered Joaquín, stumbling into the monastery.

Ana followed him.

'In the basket?' Don Cristobal frowned. 'Does your father not know about this?'

Ana interrupted him. 'Our father doesn't want him to be seen on the street,' she lied emphatically.

'Is that so?' Don Cristobal asked Joaquín.

Hanging his head, Joaquín muttered his agreement. He didn't want the monk to see his red face. He put the basket down, and Ana helped Bartolomé out. She could feel her little brother shaking with excitement. She held him good and tight so that he could lean his body against her.

'I'm Don Cristobal, and you must be Bartolomé,' said Don Cristobal, trying to hide his shock. He hadn't expected the child to be so badly deformed. The big hump, which forced his upper body forward, the crooked legs, which seemed too weak to support even the little dwarf body, the club feet. Don Cristobal felt a shudder running up his spine. He had once seen pictures of the devil which showed Satan with feet deformed like these. No, this was superstitious thinking, unworthy of a man of the cloth.

'I want so much to learn to read and write.' Bartolomé looked trustingly at Don Cristobal.

How could this ugly dwarf have such a pure, bell-like voice? Don Cristobal looked into Bartolomé's crooked face and saw something else that was wonderful: Bartolomé's eyes gleamed hopefully at him like two dark pearls. Don Cristobal went down on one knee and grasped Bartolomé's outstretched hands. These, he discovered to his surprise, were finely formed. Perhaps Joaquín was right, and God's grace rested even on this poor freak. Were the voice, the eyes and these hands not a sign?

'You will learn to read and write, Bartolomé,' promised Don Cristobal in a firm voice.

The monk led Bartolomé into the shady cloister where he had set up a low bench and a footstool under the white stone arcade. Don Cristobal sat down on the bench. When his pupil had taken up his place on the stool, the monk took a little wooden board out of his habit, on which he had carefully painted the lower-case and capital letters of the alphabet. He showed them to Bartolomé.

'This is an A, this is a B, a C ...'

Bartolomé listened carefully. Out of the corner of his eye, he could see Joaquín, weeding the roses in the courtyard.

The monk continued patiently, moving his finger over the board and naming the letters. Bartolomé repeated what was said and tried to remember the shapes of the letters.

'What is this letter called?' Don Cristobal tested him after a while.

Bartolomé stared at the straight white stroke out of which two fat tummies grew. He wasn't quite sure. All these letters looked so alike, but had such different names.

'That's a B,' he decided eventually.

Don Cristobal smiled. The crippled child was quick. In no time he had memorised all the letters on the board.

'Name the letters as I point them out,' Don Cristobal continued. His finger jumped hither and thither and Bartolomé worked hard to read the letters.

'B – A – R – T – O – L – O – M – E.'

'That's right,' Don Cristobal praised him. 'But do you know what you have just read to me?'

Bartolomé shook his head shyly. The different sounds of the letters were whirling around in his head. They didn't make any sense.

'Listen more carefully as you say them,' Don Cristobal told him, and once again, his finger wandered from letter to letter.

'B – A – R – T – O – L – O – M – E.' The dwarf looked up in astonishment. 'It sounds like my name. It sounds like Bartolomé!'

He moved his finger eagerly over the board.

'First a B, then A, R, T ...' He spelt Bartolomé without a single mistake. His name.

Don Cristobal was delighted.

'You've done very well. We'll practise some more in the next lesson.'

Bartolomé could hardly believe that his first lesson was over so quickly. But the church clock chimed the hour, confirming Don Cristobal's guess about the time.

With difficulty Bartolomé tore his eyes from the wooden board. He wanted to read more. He wanted to read Joaquín, Ana, Manuel and Beatríz. He wanted to spell butter, egg and cheese.

'Could I take the board home with me?' he asked.

Don Cristobal hesitated. He'd made the little board himself. But a monk was not allowed to own anything. Everything belonged to the monastery. On the other hand, the child would be able to practise at home if he had it, and nobody in the monastery had any use for the board.

'You must bring it back for the next lesson,' he said.

Bartolomé hugged the board to his body.

Reading and Writing

HE practised away at home. Isabel looked at her little son with a new respect. After a single lesson he was able to spell not only his own name, but also those of his brothers and sisters and his parents. She was so engrossed, she almost failed to hear Juan coming home. Quickly, she hid the letter board under Bartolomé's sleeping mat.

'You can only use it when nobody can see.'

Bartolomé knew what that meant. His father must not find out, and neither must Beatríz. She was too small to keep a secret. He sat in a corner and thought about the wonderful board. If he closed his eyes, he could see the letters in his mind. He was surprised to find that he didn't need the board. 'They're all in my head,' he whispered. He traced them in the air with his finger.

He had an idea. Impatiently, he waited till he heard his father fastening the shutters. Then he stood up and wobbled into the front room. There was a basket of coal beside the stove. He sat down quietly beside it and blackened his index finger with coal dust. Nobody took any notice of him. Isabel and Ana were preparing supper. Beatríz was playing with Manuel. Juan and Joaquín were talking and carefully brushing Juan's coachman's boots.

Bartolomé spat on the stone floor and polished it with the cuff of his shirt until it shone. Carefully he drew the letters, one after another, with his blackened finger.

Ana saw what Bartolomé was doing. She looked over at her father. Juan hadn't noticed anything. She put her foot quickly on the letters and rubbed them into smudges.

'Stop that,' she whispered to her brother. 'He mustn't get a hint of what is going on.'

Bartolomé nodded obediently, but his face was hot with joy.

'Did you see? I can write them all by myself. It's easy. They're just lines and loops.'

The next few days passed as if in a dream. In Bartolomé's head, the letters floated in and out of each other. He tried to shape them into words. Every minute that his father and Beatríz were out, he wrote words on the floor of the back room with a coal. Isabel gave him a bowl of water and a cloth.

'You must wipe them away immediately,' she warned him, and in the evenings, before Juan came home, she herself washed Bartolomé's coal-blackened hands and face. She put a clean shirt on him also and stuck the dirty one in the laundry basket.

'Ana will wash it on Saturday,' she said.

'Saturday,' thought Bartolomé. That was when he would see Don Cristobal again. He could hardly wait to climb into the laundry basket.

ASTONISHED, Don Cristobal watched the dwarf eagerly writing words on the flagged floor of the cloister, using a piece of coal. Of course, what he wrote was full of mistakes, but the letters were beautifully formed, the lines all straight and the loops regularly drawn. A slate and slate pencil lay on the bench beside the monk. Don Cristobal had intended to introduce Bartolomé to the art of writing as he had learned it himself as a young monk in the monastery's scriptorium. For days at a time, they'd had to draw nice tidy lines side by side and then later they were allowed to link them up with loops, and only when the master decided they were good and ready were they allowed to copy letters. But this child had mastered in four days what it had taken Don Cristobal ages to accomplish in his youth.

'Don Cristobal?' Bartolomé interrupted the monk's thoughts.

'Yes, my son?'

'How many words are there?'

'An infinite number.'

'Infinite. Is that as many as there are stars in the heavens?' Bartolomé was thinking of the night sky over the village.

'Even more than that,' said Don Cristobal with a smile.

Bartolomé looked at the words at his feet. How few there were, and how many he still had to learn! He couldn't imagine knowing more words than there were stars in the sky. He'd started his second lesson with the intention of learning to write everything. Now he realised how stupid that had been. He looked up unhappily at Don Cristobal.

'I'll never do it. No matter how hard I think, I just don't know enough words.'

'You'll learn them.'

'How?'

Don Cristobal made a decision.

'Wait here.' He hurried away through the cloisters. He was back in a moment. In his hand he had a fat leather-bound book.

'Sit up beside me on the bench,' he ordered Bartolomé.

Bartolomé clambered up. Being so twisted in his body, he needed to lean against the monk in order to be able to look into the book.

Don Cristobal leafed carefully through the pages. They were all filled with closely written letters.

'As many as the stars in the sky,' Bartolomé thought. There had to be an infinite number of words in this book. As Don Cristobal stopped turning the pages and put a finger on one line, Bartolomé bent forward eagerly. He would read all these words, he thought, he would take note of them, and later he would transcribe them using a piece of coal.

'In those days ...' Bartolomé stumbled from word to word. Sometimes, a word was too long for him, and then Don Cristobal had to help him to sound out the letters in the right order so that they yielded up their sense. Suddenly Bartolomé stopped.

'I know this story. It's the Christmas story,' he realised, surprised.

Don Cristobal nodded in agreement. 'So now you know what book I have been reading from?'

Bartolomé looked reverently at the book. It had to be the Bible. At home in the village, only Father Rodriguez had read the Bible.

'I don't want ... I can't become a priest,' stammered Bartolomé, shocked.

Don Cristobal suppressed a laugh. 'People who are not priests can read the Bible too,' he explained with a smile.

Bartolomé gave a sigh of relief and bent over the page again. Now that he knew which story it was, he managed to read it far more easily. Sometimes he could even work out a long word by himself.

In the end, Don Cristobal put a hand over the page, hiding it.

'Now you must write the words too, Bartolomé. You need to look at them carefully, letter by letter, and then afterwards you'll write them from memory.'

Bartolomé slithered off the bench and knelt on the ground. He took the slate and the slate pencil from Don Cristobal. Then the monk held the Bible for him and showed him a word.

'K-neel,' Bartolomé read.

'Kneel,' the monk corrected him.

There were only a few letters in the word. It couldn't be that hard. First came a K ... But wait a minute.

'Why is there a K that is not pronounced in that word?' he asked.

'For the look of it,' answered the monk. 'Sometimes a letter is just there so that the word looks right, but it's not pronounced. That is the beauty of the written word.'

'But that's so hard!' said Bartolomé. He thought about the words he'd written out at home on the floor. He'd just written them according to the way they sounded to him, because he didn't know about this beauty thing.

'Did I make a lot of mistakes?' asked Bartolomé, meaning the words he'd written on the flags at the beginning of the lesson.

'An awful lot,' said Don Cristobal merrily. But when he saw how horrified Bartolomé was, he added: 'You'll soon come to recognise the words by reading and then you'll be able to write them without making any mistakes.'

Reading, thought Bartolomé. Would Don Cristobal lend him the Bible? He stretched out his hand automatically for it. Don Cristobal shook his head.

'That won't do, Bartolomé. The Bible belongs to the monastery. I can't lend it.'

'But I brought the board back!'

'Yes, but you can see that the Bible is worth a lot more than a homemade alphabet board,' said Don Cristobal kindly.

Disappointed, Bartolomé stared at the book. If he wasn't going to be allowed to read it, he would never learn to write properly.

'Your father should buy you a cheaper book,' the monk suggested. 'Then you can practise your reading and writing at home.'

Bartolomé was just about to shake his head sadly and explain to the monk how unlikely it was that his father, of all people, would buy him a book. Just in time, he remembered that Don Cristobal did not know the whole truth.

'I'll ask him,' muttered Bartolomé.

Don Cristobal nodded contentedly.

'Next week, you can show me your own book, and we'll use it to practise on. The Bible belongs in the library and I can't borrow it a second time without the abbot's permission.'

A Book

'I NEED a book,' Bartolomé announced as soon as Isabel hauled him out of the laundry basket.

'A book?' Isabel looked at Bartolomé in dismay. Only priests and rich people had books, people who had mastered the art of reading and who had the means. Simple people like them didn't own books.

'The Bible would be best.' Bartolomé was thinking of Don Cristobal's fat book that contained infinitely many words.

'The Bible!' cried Isabel in horror. A Bible cost a small fortune. She remembered that they had collected money in the village to buy a new Bible when Father Rodriguez's old Bible had become illegible because it was covered with spots of mildew. Every family had had to contribute.

'You can forget about that,' she said shortly and began hanging up the wet clothes.

'I can't make any progress without a book,' said Bartolomé stubbornly.

'But you're able to read and write already. Take a piece of coal. I'll say all the words I can think of, and you can write them out.'

'I can't,' sighed Bartolomé dejectedly.

Isabel left her washing and hunkered down in front of Bartolomé. She stroked his hair.

'Nonsense. Yesterday, you could write anything.'

'It wasn't right. It was only the sound, and not the way the words are spelt,' Bartolomé tried to explain. 'It's only when you know the spellings that you can write the words without mistakes.'

Isabel didn't understand what Bartolomé was talking about. 'Don Cristobal will teach you these spellings in the next lesson, and you'll remember them,' she said consolingly.

Bartolomé laughed, in spite of himself.

'You see? Everything is fine again,' said Isabel happily, making to go back to her work.

Bartolomé grabbed hold of her. 'Mama,' he asked, 'did you ever count the stars in the sky?'

'Of course not. You can't do that. There are too many.'

'If every star was not a light but was a word, would you be able to learn all those words, without looking at the sky?'

Isabel looked attentively at Bartolomé. 'You mean,' she said slowly, 'that you don't just have to hear words, you have to see them if you want to be able to write them down?'

Bartolomé nodded. 'That's the way it is. I learned that today. And that's why Don Cristobal wants me to have my own book, so I can learn the spellings of the words out of it. He can't give me one, and I can't ask Papa.'

Isabel put her arm around Bartolomé. Where was she going to get a book for him? She needed the few coins she earned from her sewing for the housekeeping. She'd only been able to pay for the two little candles that Bartolomé's lessons cost by buying vegetables at the market for herself and the children that were not as fresh as they should have been. She could use that to make a thick soup and along with the stale bread that Joaquín could get cheaply from the baker, she could fill the children's tummies.

Beatríz and Manuel were too small to notice the difference. Joaquín, Ana and Bartolomé didn't complain, because they knew what Isabel was saving the money for. *But it will never be enough for a whole book,* thought Isabel.

'We can't do it, Bartolomé,' she whispered, hugging him tightly.

Ana, who until now had been sitting in a corner, listening, got up and went to them. 'I know a way out,' she said decisively.

Isabel stood up. 'What's that?' she asked.

'When Señora Lopez and Maria go to the apothecary shop in the mornings, I can sneak a book down. The widow has a few in her bedroom. I can make sure that Teresa and Gaspar suspect nothing. Then, before the widow comes home, I can put the book back.'

Bartolomé beamed. He had never loved Ana so much as he did just at that moment.

Isabel looked horrified. 'That's stealing,' she said.

Ana shrugged her shoulders. 'Bartolomé needs a book, and we're just borrowing one for him.'

'But taking something without asking is stealing,' replied Isabel.

'It's a question of Bartolomé's future. We have to do it,' Ana insisted.

'No!' Isabel knew she could never approve of theft. If only she owned something that she could swap for a book! She thought of the little wooden box with her jewellery in it. There were just a few cheap pieces of thin silver. Only her grandmother's ring was worth anything. It was gold, with a sparkling chip of diamond. She might get enough money for it to buy a book. On the other hand, it was an heirloom, destined for Ana, just as she, as the eldest daughter, had got the ring from her mother on her deathbed.

'My ring,' said Isabel softly.

Ana understood at once what she meant. She knew the piece of jewellery and had often admired it. One day, the ring would be hers. Not to wear, of course, but to treasure as a valuable jewel, as her mother did.

Ana hesitated. The ring for a book? Maybe Don Cristobal could still be persuaded to lend Bartolomé one. Or maybe he'd got it wrong, and Bartolomé could learn to spell even without a book? And why couldn't she secretly borrow one of Señora Lopez's books in her absence? That would hurt nobody, whereas the ring would be lost for ever. Had Bartolomé any idea how hard and how unfair this decision was?

'Ana, if I get work and it makes me rich, the first thing I will do is buy you a new ring,' Bartolomé promised.

Ana looked into her brother's dark eyes. 'We'll sell the ring,' she agreed.

'Do you really want to do that?' Isabel asked.

Ana nodded quickly.

Isabel got the jewellery box from the back room and gave it to her eldest daughter. Carefully, Ana opened the lid and put the ring on her finger. She went to the window and held it up to the sunlight. It glittered. Dreamily, Ana waved the ring back and forth. She would never own this piece of jewellery now.

'What are you doing?' asked Joaquín, coming in and putting down a leather water container. It was one of his chores to fetch water every day, and since Isabel never pressed him to come home quickly, he liked doing it. He liked wandering through the narrow streets of Madrid, observing the merchants and the artisans or running along behind a fine coach along with other lads in the hope that the rich owner would take a notion and throw them a few coins, which they would then jostle for.

On this afternoon, however, his rumbling stomach had brought him home earlier than usual.

'Why have you put that ring on? Joaquín asked now.

'We're going to use it to buy a book for Bartolomé,' Isabel explained.

It took Joaquín a while to work out what was going on. Like Ana, he was of the opinion that she should use Señora Lopez's books. Isabel absolutely forbade it. None of her children could ever have theft on their conscience.

'Don't sell the ring, though,' Joaquín suggested. 'Pawn it.'

Isabel blenched. Only the very poorest people went to the pawn shop. It was a terrible shame for a family when a person was forced to pawn their possessions.

'Then I can redeem the ring later, and give it back to Ana!' cried Bartolomé, delighted.

'But suppose I don't get enough money that way to buy a book,' Isabel asked.

'Don't take any money for the ring,' explained Joaquín. 'Instead, ask for a book. In Calle Granado there is a pawnbroker who sometimes sits out in front of his shop, reading. He'd definitely agree to that plan. And when Bartolomé doesn't need the book any more, we can take it back and then all we have to pay is the interest. That can't be too bad.'

'How do you know all this?' asked Ana.

'You can learn a lot in this city if you are quick on your feet and if you keep your eyes open and your wits about you,' Joaquín answered, very sure of himself.

Isabel wrapped the ring in a piece of linen and hid it carefully in her petticoat pocket. Draping her scarf over her head and shoulders, she turned to Ana.

'Go and get Beatríz and Manuel from downstairs and stay here with them in the apartment,' she ordered.

Ana nodded.

'And get the supper ready.'

'What if Papa comes home earlier than usual?' asked Ana.

Isabel hesitated. Juan must never know that she'd gone to the pawnbroker. On the other hand, she couldn't lie to him.

'Joaquín, take the little jug with you. We'll buy some oil at the market,' she said.

Ana smiled. 'So you've gone out to buy oil,' she said.

Isabel reddened. 'That's right,' she snapped.

The Pawnbroker

CALLE GRANADO was one of those alleyways where dark little workshops were huddled among the shops. Smiths, cobblers, weavers, coopers, potters, bakers and butchers were all squashed in together. The baker quarrelled with the butcher about his waste which attracted rats. The weaver complained loudly about the suffocating smoke that poured out of the smith's and got into his cloth. The shoemaker was poor and could only afford to use substandard leather, and he remained poor because his customers would pay only small amounts for shoes like that. The cooper's big wooden barrels were rattled carelessly over the bockety cobbles by his two apprentices and made the potter fear for the safety of his wares which he had set out in front of his doorway.

The pawnbroker's shop was at the end of the street.

At last, thought Joaquín, *I have a chance to see what is behind the locked door decorated with three gold-painted balls.*

The pawnbroker was an old man with a white beard, dressed in black. As usual, he was sitting on a chair in front of his door, reading. The fact that someone could earn his living by sitting in idleness, reading, impressed Joaquín.

'I can't do it,' Isabel whispered to him as they stood outside the shop. She was embarrassed to think that all the passersby would be whispering about her.

Joaquín stepped up to the pawnbroker. 'Señor, my mother would like to pledge a ring for a short while,' he said politely.

The old man snapped his book shut and stood up. 'Everything that is left here is left only for a short time, Señora,' he said kindly.

He opened the door and led Isabel and Joaquín into a dusky room. 'Rebecca!' he called. 'We have customers.'

A pretty young girl emerged from the darkness, carrying an oil lamp. She put it down on a table and smiled at Joaquín and Isabel. Isabel rummaged in her skirt. With shaking fingers, she took out the ring and unwrapped it. She held the jewel out to Joaquín, who put it on the table. The pawnbroker pushed the oil lamp nearer. He took a magnifying glass and a pair of scales out of a drawer. He weighed the ring carefully and examined it closely for a long time.

'Definitely more than one generation old,' he murmured. 'Comes from the Seville area, if I am not mistaken.'

Joaquín stared at the girl. She had an ivory face, framed by jet-black hair.

'Rebecca, offer the señora a seat,' ordered the pawnbroker.

Isabel protested, but Rebecca pushed a chair towards her. Joaquín put out his hand for it.

'Thank you very much, Señorita,' he said hoarsely.

Isabel sat down. Her hands were clutching the linen that the ring had been wrapped in. Suppose the pawnbroker put the ring in his pocket and sent them away without giving them anything for it!

The old man stretched his back. 'The ring has a certain value,' he declared carefully, watching the woman's face closely. Interpreting the relief that always showed in the faces of customers when this sentence was pronounced was an art

71

in itself. That was how he managed always to lend just as much money as the customer needed, and not as much as the jewellery was actually worth. If they could pay him back the sum lent later, he pocketed only the small amount of interest. On the other hand, it often happened that he made a hefty profit if the piece had not been reclaimed by the agreed time and so reverted to him.

Isabel cast her eyes down. She felt uncomfortable under the gaze of the old man. She was afraid of him.

Joaquín stood in front of his mother. 'We want to swap the ring for a book,' he said bravely, 'preferably the Bible.'

Bartolomé had insisted to him that only the Bible contained infinitely many words.

'The ring for a book?' repeated the pawnbroker disbelievingly.

Joaquín nodded. 'My brother needs it to study reading and writing. When he's mastered it, we'll bring the book back and get the ring.'

The pawnbroker shook his head. Never before had anyone suggested such an unusual trade. 'If I give you a book, you'll have to pay the interest in cash.'

Joaquín nodded his agreement.

'Within six months – by Epiphany, that is – you must redeem the ring. Otherwise, it's mine.'

'Agreed, Señor.'

Joaquín put out his hand, relieved, to seal the bargain.

'Just a minute,' said the pawnbroker. 'I haven't got a Bible. But I have other fat books. Rebecca, get them out of the chest.'

Joaquín thought things over. Bartolomé wanted a Bible. The pawnbroker had only other books. How was he going to know which of them was good enough for studying out of?

Rebecca came back with an armful of leather volumes and put them down beside the ring on the table. They smelt musty.

'Choose one,' the pawnbroker urged Joaquín.

Joaquín bit his lip. Should he just take the thickest book?

'They are good books,' said the girl softly.

Joaquín looked at her in surprise. Could she read?

'Joaquín, make a decision,' Isabel whispered behind him. 'We have to go.' The sooner she could get out of this dark room, the better.

'Which book has the most words in it?' asked Joaquín uncertainly.

The old man raised his eyebrows. 'A good story doesn't have to have a lot of words, and bad stories can be written in way too many sentences,' he said, a little snootily.

Joaquín felt his cheeks burning, and he was glad that his face couldn't be seen here in this dim light. 'My brother doesn't need the book for pleasure, Señor, but in order to learn to spell as many words as possible,' he explained.

The pawnbroker snorted audibly. 'Then take the thickest.'

'Father!' said the girl quietly. She bent over the books and quickly pulled one out. It wasn't the thickest book, Joaquín could see, and the leather was stained.

'*Don Quixote*, by Cervantes,' said the girl. 'You can study this book for days and it is still enjoyable to read the story. It makes you laugh and it makes you cry.' She offered it to Joaquín.

Can a book really make someone laugh and cry? Joaquín wondered, holding it awkwardly in his hands.

At home, Bartolomé received it with great excitement. His own book, even if only for a short while. He sniffed. The printed paper smelt strangely of old cellars.

'It's not the Bible,' Joaquín admitted. 'The pawnbroker didn't have one. But his daughter recommended this. She can read.'

Bartolomé riffled through the pages with his fingers. The book seemed to have just as many words as Don Cristobal's Bible. And it had pictures. Delighted, Bartolomé looked at the engravings. A lean man on a horse, holding in his hand a lance that was way too long. In the background stood a couple of windmills.

'Don Quixote, a knight of sorry appearance, fights windmills,' Bartolomé spelt out.

Why would anyone fight windmills? How come this man, who didn't look a bit aristocratic but more like a fool, was a knight? And why was he of sorry appearance? Bartolomé couldn't see any deformities in his body. Forgetting all about Isabel, Ana and Joaquín, he opened the first page and started to read under his breath. It wasn't easy. The long words made Bartolomé feel as if his tongue was in a knot when he tried to put the sounds together in the proper order. But the story of Don Quixote captivated him. He read on, page after page.

'He read,' Bartolomé murmured, 'day and night, and because he read too much and ate too little, the fluids in his brain dried out and he lost his reason.'

Isabel gave a shout of horror. She'd been listening spellbound to the extraordinary story for an hour. Now she had her doubts. Could a person lose their reason through reading?

'Shut that book, Bartolomé!' she cried.

Bartolomé looked up, baffled. He'd completely forgotten that he was sitting on his sleeping mat. In his thoughts, he had been in that little town where Don Quixote had his house.

'Look, you're all in a muddle. Put it aside. Joaquín will take it back tomorrow. We might not even have to pay any interest.'

Bartolomé hugged the leather volume close. He wouldn't let her do that to him. He needed the book. 'It's only a story,' he said. 'Somebody just made it up. It's not necessarily true.'

'But if it is?' asked Isabel. 'Suppose you go mad. Is it not bad enough that you ...' She stopped.

'He can show it to Don Cristobal at the next lesson,' said Ana into the silence. '*He'll* know if it's dangerous to read it.'

'Until then, you are not even to look at those pages! Promise me that?' Isabel crouched down to Bartolomé.

Bartolomé agreed unwillingly. He wouldn't see Don Cristobal again until Tuesday. He'd lose so many hours. Precious time when he should be practising reading and writing.

'Bartolomé, look me in the eye and promise me loud and clear.'

'Yes.' Bartolomé watched unhappily as Isabel took the book from his reluctant hands and stuck it into a cloth bag. She hid the bag in a chest.

'Sometimes,' she grumbled, 'I think all these secrets will end in tears. Maybe we should let your father in on it. He'd know for sure what's best for Bartolomé.'

'No!' cried Ana, Joaquín and Bartolomé together.

'When Bartolomé can put the first money he has earned himself on the table, then Papa can know,' said Joaquín firmly.

Otherwise, he'll send me back to the village, to Tomáz, thought Bartolomé.

And he wouldn't be able to bear that.

Pen and Ink

AFTER the last lesson, Don Cristobal, whose conscience was bothering him, went to the abbot to get his permission to teach Bartolomé. The monastery was small, with only a few monks, and the abbot was a kindly man. When Don Cristobal told him about Joaquín's impassioned plea and about Bartolomé's eagerness to learn, the abbot forgave him his unauthorised behaviour and allowed the monk to teach Bartolomé, as long as he did not neglect his duties. Don Cristobal promised that he wouldn't.

When Joaquín and Bartolomé came to the monastery on the following Tuesday, Don Cristobal had an altar to prepare in the church for a mass. Joaquín offered to help with that. Bartolomé remained in the cloister on his own, sitting waiting on a wooden footstool, leaning his hump against the cool white stone wall. He opened his cloth bag and took out the book. Could it really be dangerous to read? For two long days he'd kept staring at the chest in which the book was hidden. Dozens of times a day, he'd love to have taken it out and read on. Even now, his fingers were itching. They wanted to leaf through the pages. How long was it going to take until Don Cristobal came back from the church?

Insects hummed among the roses. In the little garden that was surrounded by the cloister, the sun warmed Bartolomé's face. A breeze ruffled his hair and rustled the pages of the book.

Bartolomé decided to open the page with the worrisome sentence on it, not to read it, but to show it to Don Cristobal as soon as he had finished his work. Bartolomé's fingers hovered over the lines. He read a word here and there. At last, he found the place he was looking for. 'And lost his reason,' Bartolomé read. His eyes followed the sentence. Without meaning to, or maybe because he really did mean it, he read on.

There were many words that he could not decipher. People's names, words in a foreign language, expressions that he didn't know. But every line he read led him further into the story of this extraordinary, slightly mad knight. Bartolomé could almost see Don Quixote polishing up and putting on his grandfather's armour, saddling his skinny horse and giving him a new name: Rosinante.

'What's that book you are reading?'

Bartolomé started with fright. Don Cristobal had come back and was bending down to him, so that the folds of his brown habit covered the book.

'I didn't mean to keep reading,' Bartolomé stammered.

'Why not? I am pleased when my pupil is diligent.'

'Because … because I don't know if, if, if …' Bartolomé, still half-lost in the story, was searching for words.

Don Cristobal waited patiently.

'My mother thinks that you can lose your reason by reading this book,' Bartolomé explained at last.

'Lose your reason? Where ever did she get an idea like that?'

Bartolomé could hear in Don Cristobal's voice what a stupid idea he thought that was. He was ashamed on his mother's behalf. At the same time, he wanted to stick up for her, silly as she was.

'It says so here.' He leafed quickly back and put his finger on the fatal line. Don Cristobal read it thoughtfully, once, then a second time.

'I know this book,' he said. 'A fantastic story. Cervantes was a great author. But he's not reporting reality. It's all made up.'

Bartolomé felt relieved.

'So reading doesn't make you mad?' he asked.

Don Cristobal hesitated. He couldn't entirely rule it out. 'Of course, it could happen,' he said thoughtfully, 'that if a person like Don Quixote did nothing but read nonsense and forgot to work, forgot to eat and sleep and pray, he might possibly lose his reason because of it.'

'And this book, is it nonsense?' asked Bartolomé, wanting to know exactly what was what.

Don Cristobal shook his head. 'No. It's fantasy, not nonsense.'

'I don't understand that,' Bartolomé admitted. For him, they were the same thing.

'At the royal court, there are jesters and fools,' explained Don Cristobal. 'The jester wears motley, and everyone laughs at him. But the fool, on the other hand, dresses up his jibes with folly and in this way hides the point of his jokes from the audience. They mock him anyway. But if they are smart, they realise that the fool has held up a mirror to them, and then they laugh at themselves, not at the fool.'

'Don Quixote, is he a fool?' asked Bartolomé, thinking it over.

'Cervantes is the fool. He makes Don Quixote do all the stupid things that we ourselves do all too often. So you should not just study the words, but also think about the meaning of the story. In that way, your reason, far from being lost, is developed.'

'I'll do that,' Bartolomé promised eagerly.

Don Cristobal smiled. How wonderful it was that even in this body that would always remain small and crooked, there was something that could grow into greatness. *He'll surprise us all yet*, he thought confidently.

The monk sat down beside Bartolomé and together they started to read. Patiently, Don Cristobal explained the expressions that Bartolomé didn't know. He pointed out to him unusual spellings which seemed to go against the sounds of the words. He made his pupil, who was thirsty for knowledge, write out the hard words on his slate. Bartolomé was so keen, he didn't notice the time passing. He was sad when the clocks all chimed the hour and the monk finished the lesson, because now he would have to wait another four days.

Don Cristobal noticed Bartolomé's sadness. Against his better judgement, he ran quickly into the library, and out of the big oak cupboard he took a few sheets of paper, a quill pen and a little flask of ink. He'd have to confess this theft to the abbot some time.

In the cloister, he gave Bartolomé the utensils. 'You can use these to study at home. Any time you come across something that you don't understand, make a note of it. The next time you come, I'll answer all your questions.'

Bartolomé's eyes shone with joy as he carefully placed his quill, ink and paper in the cloth bag. Now he had what a secretary needed. Don Cristobal looked at the dwarf. *Even if I am not forgiven for the theft*, he thought to himself, *I'd still do it again.*

'Thank you,' whispered Bartolomé, overcome, and put his arms out to embrace Don Cristobal. The monk hugged him briefly. Through his habit he could feel the beating of Bartolomé's heart.

As the door closed behind the children, Don Cristobal realised that he felt as if he had just embraced a perfect body.

At home, Isabel stared at the paper, quill and ink. She could not take it all in, that her little crippled Bartolomé possessed these fine things.

'Are you really going to use it?' she asked.

Bartolomé looked up from his book and gave a scholarly nod. 'If there is something that I don't understand, I'll write it down,' he explained. His face glowing with joy, he smoothed out a sheet of paper, opened his inkpot, dunked the quill in it, tapped the drops carefully from it, and formed letters on the paper.

'Don Quixote,' he wrote as a heading. Under that, he was going to make a list of all the words that he could not make out.

'You'd better get rid of it pretty sharpish before Papa or Beatríz comes home,' Isabel warned him.

Bartolomé nodded. But within moments, he was so engrossed in his work that he didn't notice Isabel starting to get supper ready. It was only when she laid her hand gently on his hump that he noticed the smell of cooking. Reluctantly, he put everything away in the chest. *If only morning would come,* thought Bartolomé longingly.

Joaquín Goes Away

BARTOLOMÉ was so lost in thought during supper that Ana kicked him surreptitiously. 'Pull yourself together,' she whispered. 'Papa has looked over at you three times because you're not eating and are staring into space.'

Hastily, Bartolomé stuck a piece of bread into his mouth and chewed on it.

'I have good news,' said Juan proudly.

Everyone looked expectantly at him.

'It has to do with Joaquín. I spoke to the baker today. He is very satisfied. After dinner, Joaquín and I are going to go over there to sign the contract. From tomorrow, you'll be an apprentice baker.'

Bartolomé could see how pleased Joaquín was about the praise and about his father's pride. *When I can read and write properly*, Bartolomé thought, *he'll be proud of me too.*

'I'll miss him,' said Isabel. 'He's saved me a lot of work.'

Juan nodded. 'It's time Beatríz began to help more around the house. She's old enough now.'

Beatríz pulled a face and sulked. She didn't want to work. Playing was much nicer.

'I could sew by the time I was six,' Ana pointed out to her little sister. In her opinion, Beatríz had been far too spoilt.

As if turned to stone, Bartolomé sat among them. Was he the only one who realised how dreadful this change was going to be? Joaquín was going to move out, and Beatríz was going to be home more to help out around the house instead of playing in the yard. How was he going to study and – he shuddered – how was he going to get to Don Cristobal if Joaquín couldn't carry him? Bartolomé's arms and legs started to shake. He could feel Juan staring at him crossly. But he couldn't stop. The muscles in his face clenched, making it even more crooked. A little thread of spittle ran out of the corner of his mouth.

'Go to bed,' said Juan in disgust.

Isabel jumped up and carried Bartolomé into the little bedroom. She rolled out his sleeping mat, laid him on it, and covered his shivering body. 'He'll come to visit us as soon as he can,' she said to console him.

Bartolomé turned his face away from her. Visit! He needed Joaquín's swift legs and his strong back. Without him, he couldn't manage.

Juan stood in the doorway. 'I knew that Madrid was no place for Bartolomé. At home, he never shook like this. As soon as I get permission, I will go back to the village and take him with me.'

Isabel said nothing. Even through the cover, she could see how her son was still shivering. In the village Bartolomé had been different and she had had no secrets from her husband. Maybe it would be better for everyone if Bartolomé went back there after all.

The next morning Joaquín stood awkwardly beside Bartolomé's sleeping mat. 'I'm leaving now, Bartolomé,' he said. He was carrying a bundle with his clothes wrapped in it under his right arm.

Bartolomé had refused to get up and have breakfast.

'When he gets hungry, he'll come,' Juan had said and wouldn't let Isabel get him.

It's all gone so quickly since supper last night, thought Joaquín, looking at the silent shape under the bedclothes. He'd hardly have thought it possible that he would be going this morning to the baker with his father. Nobody in his family had ever learnt a trade before. They'd all been poor tenant farmers. Joaquín was planning to become the best baker in Madrid. Maybe he would even supply the royal court.

Bartolomé knew he should say goodbye to Joaquín. He would only see him occasionally in the coming years. But at that moment, he hated his brother.

Has Joaquín no idea how much damage he is doing? thought Bartolomé bitterly. Joaquín could just as easily go to learn his trade and start his own life later. But because he was going now, he was destroying Bartolomé's only hope of achieving the same. He didn't want to talk to Joaquín or even to look at him.

Joaquín hunkered down beside the mat. 'I'm sorry,' he whispered. 'But this was always the plan. You knew all along I was on probation with the baker and that I was going to have to go and live there when the apprenticeship was set up.'

Joaquín stroked the cover unhappily. He didn't want Bartolomé to be sad. 'And anyway, you can read now,' he said.

Bartolomé stiffened.

'I'll go and explain to Don Cristobal why you can't come any more, so he won't think you're just lazy,' Joaquín promised.

Bartolomé didn't move.

'I'm sure you can keep the paper and the pen and ink for a while longer. You can use those things to practise your writing.

You're so smart, Bartolomé. You'll do it, even without Don Cristobal's help. I know you will.'

Bartolomé suppressed a sob.

'As soon as I get a day off, I'll take you and your paper with all the questions on it to Don Cristobal. I promise.'

Joaquín stood up and waited. Bartolomé didn't answer. He gave no indication of having heard a word of what Joaquín had said.

'I helped you as much as I could,' said Joaquín, crestfallen. 'You never once said thank you.'

Now the cover moved and Bartolomé stuck out a tear-stained face. His mouth was a hard line.

'First you behave as if I am a real human being, then you just take off. You were probably lying all along.'

Bartolomé knew how unfair this accusation was. He could see how much he'd hurt Joaquín with it. Even so, he added, 'And I hate you for that. I don't want anything more from you. You can go. I don't need a brother.'

Joaquín left the room without a word.

When Bartolomé heard the front door closing, he started to cry and cry. He wished he could run after Joaquín.

Ana came in and sat down beside Bartolomé on the floor. To console him, she took his head on her lap. She ruffled his hair softly with her hand. She sang a tune that she had made up herself. Gradually, Bartolomé's sobs died down. And in the end, he stopped crying.

'If you promise me,' whispered Ana, 'that you will work away on your own for two weeks, then I'll try to find a way to get you to Don Cristobal in the laundry basket after that.'

Bartolomé sat up. 'The basket is too heavy,' he said. 'Joaquín is stronger than you, and even he could barely carry me. There is no point in promising me something you can't do.'

Ana's face took on a decisive look. 'Do you want to become a secretary or not?' she asked.

'Of course I do, but –'

'No buts! Take your book and start learning. Use every hour. I'll make sure that Beatríz has to go to the well for water. That'll keep her out of the way for a while.'

Bartolomé looked up at his big sister. Her voice sounded just like her father's. Did she know that?

Ana left the room and Bartolomé crawled off his mat, washed his face and hands in the washbasin, dried himself carefully and got his book, paper, ink and pen out of the chest. He opened the book and began to study. But all the time, he could see Ana's face in his mind's eye. Would she really take him to Don Cristobal?

Without giving much thought to what he was doing, Bartolomé took up a piece of paper. He dipped his pen in the ink, and wrote, 'Ana will always help me. She promised.'

Now that it was there in black and white, Bartolomé's confidence grew that she would be able to do it. But should he waste a piece of paper like this? Well, it was too late to worry about that now.

'I love Ana very much,' he added.

And Joaquín? *He left me in the lurch*, Bartolomé answered his own inner voice. But he knew that was not true.

He dipped his pen in the ink again and started to write, one sentence after another. He wrote down all his troubles from his heart. When he had finished, he felt relieved. In this way, he felt, he had somehow begged Joaquín's pardon.

The bottom one-third of the page was still blank. But no more sentences occurred to Bartolomé, so instead he drew, as he used to draw in the sand of the village square. Using light strokes, he drew Ana, consoling him; Joaquín, shouldering the laundry basket; Beatríz coming home from the well with a jug of water, scowling, and Manuel in his mother's arms.

Drawing is much easier than writing, Bartolomé thought. It allowed him to express things that he couldn't find words for. After some hesitation, he added, right in the corner, a picture of Juan putting on his uniform. And under it he wrote one final sentence: 'He must not send me back.'

It was a kind of vow. Bartolomé folded the page and stuck it into a crack in the floorboards.

Ana's Plan

OVER the next two weeks, Bartolomé studied diligently. He read page after page. Using a piece of chalk that Isabel had somehow found for him, and which did not leave smears when it was wiped out, he covered the floor of the little room with words. His list of questions also grew. Before long, he had run out of paper and his inkpot was almost empty.

At last, the fourteen days were over. When he woke up the next morning, Bartolomé looked expectantly at Ana. He was afraid to ask. He was afraid that she was not going to be able to keep her promise. But Ana gave a confident smile.

'When Beatríz goes to the market with Mama this afternoon, then it's time,' she whispered happily into his ear, as if there was no question of a problem.

The morning dragged by endlessly in the little room. Bartolomé had scrubbed his face ages ago and combed his wild hair and changed his shirt. He had his bundle of papers stacked up neatly and placed in the cloth bag along with his book, paper, pen and ink. He waited, listening. He could still hear Beatríz's light voice and Isabel's soft, deep one in the living room. When would they go? Noon had just chimed. At last, just as he was about to explode with impatience, he heard the door shutting and Ana came into the little bedroom. She had the laundry basket on her back.

'You can't carry me,' said Bartolomé, disappointed. 'You're not able for it.'

'Wait and see. Don't be so curious,' answered Ana mysteriously.

She didn't often get a chance to hatch a plan and carry it out. That was not the kind of thing a young girl did, one that might soon be getting married. All the more reason to enjoy making Bartolomé wait a bit.

'Come down with me,' she said, helping him to the front door of the apartment. At this hour, she could be sure there'd be nobody on the stairs.

Bartolomé followed Ana down the steep, dark stairs. He slithered from step to step on his bottom. Downstairs in the dim hallway, Ana put the laundry basket down in front of Don Zorillo's door, helped Bartolomé into it, and covered him carefully with a few pieces of washing.

'Keep still and don't make a sound.'

She knocked on the door. Doña Rosita opened it.

'Good afternoon,' said Ana demurely.

'Good afternoon.' Doña Rosita gave Ana a slightly worried look. Manuel was with her, and she was afraid that Ana had come to fetch him.

'I wonder if I could take Jeronima with me to do the laundry,' Ana asked.

Doña Rosita smiled, relieved. 'Any time!' she said. 'She just sits all day in the corner and has no interest in anything, the poor thing.'

Doña Rosita took a shawl out of a chest and pulled Jeronima out from between the stove and the table. She put the shawl around her big strong daughter, who, at the age of twenty, had the mind of a four-year-old child.

Ana put out her hand. 'Come on, Jeronima, you can help me with the washing.'

Jeronima started to beam and wave her hands about excitedly. She nodded enthusiastically. She liked Ana. This girl was always nice to her.

'Promise me that you'll be good and you'll stay with Ana,' said Doña Rosita.

'I'm good,' Jeronima said quickly and followed Ana out into the hall.

As soon as the door had closed, Ana pointed to the laundry basket.

'Dear Jeronima,' she said in a flattering voice, 'you're so strong. Wouldn't you like to carry the basket for me?'

'I am very strong,' said Jeronima puffing out her chest. She bent down and Ana put the straps over her shoulders. Jeronima straightened up with no trouble. She didn't seem to feel the heavy burden.

Hand in hand, the two girls stepped out of the house into the bright sunshine. They strolled through the streets. Ana gave Jeronima lots of time to look at everything. She stood patiently with her in front of a variety of shops. Jeronima was as pleased as a child when a street juggler blocked their way and put on a little display for them. When the man looked for a tip at the end of his performance, Jeronima rummaged eagerly in her pocket, only to find nothing there.

'No money,' she said sadly.

The juggler, who had noticed that Jeronima was simple, bowed kindly, took off his multicoloured hat and said, 'For a lovely señorita like you, my show is free.'

Jeronima beamed and Ana smiled shyly at the performer.

'We have to go now,' she whispered to Jeronima. The juggler waved after them.

At last they arrived at the monastery. Ana helped Jeronima to slip out of the straps and put the laundry basket down at the door.

Jeronima looked around curiously. She frowned. 'Where is the well?' she asked.

'First I have to drop something off in the monastery,' Ana explained. 'Do you see the silversmith over there? You can go and take a look at his jewellery if you like.'

Jeronima hurried off.

Ana knocked, suddenly thinking, *Suppose Don Cristobal is not on door duty today?* But her fears came to nothing. The heavy wooden door opened and the friendly face of Don Cristobal appeared. It took him a moment to realise who the girl was. 'Where has Joaquín been all this time?' asked the monk.

Ana pushed the laundry basket past him into the interior. Quickly, she helped Bartolomé out. She had no time for answering questions. Who knew what Jeronima was getting up to at the silversmith's?

'I'm in a hurry, Father,' she said. 'I'll be back in an hour.'

She picked up the basket and ran off. When they were sitting in their usual place under the shady colonnades of the cloister, Bartolomé explained to Don Cristobal why they hadn't come for so long.

'Joaquín is a baker's apprentice now,' Bartolomé announced.

'An honourable calling. Bakers are always needed,' answered Don Cristobal.

'Secretaries also?' asked Bartolomé.

'If they are well educated and hardworking,' said Don

Cristobal with a smile. He sensed that Bartolomé was impatient to get started on the lesson.

'I am!' cried Bartolomé. He took everything proudly out of the cloth bag. 'The inkpot is empty. The paper is covered in questions. And I'm halfway through the book. I wrote out so many words that the floor of my room wasn't big enough.'

'Well, show me your questions, then,' said Don Cristobal.

Bartolomé put the bundle of paper into the monk's lap and Don Cristobal leafed through the pages. He was surprised all over again to see what lovely, regular handwriting the dwarf had. Don Cristobal studied the questions, noting that most of the words were perfectly spelt. The child had made obvious progress.

Don Cristobal patiently explained to Bartolomé all the words that he hadn't known.

'I should learn these foreign languages,' Bartolomé said as Don Cristobal translated another Latin word for him.

'Yes, I would advise you to do that. With your ability, you will have no trouble learning several languages. Perhaps you could get work as an assistant with a teacher or even with an actual secretary, and French and Latin –' Don Cristobal stopped short. He'd forgotten for a moment that Bartolomé was a crippled dwarf. Nobody would take him on as an assistant.

'I'm sorry, Bartolomé,' he said. 'I just wasn't thinking.'

'That's all right,' said Bartolomé softly. 'I know that no teacher or secretary would take me on as an apprentice. It's not so important for me to learn these languages. If I can earn my living as a letter-writer, then I'll have to be happy with that.'

'All the same, I shouldn't have forgotten,' said Don Cristobal.

Bartolomé looked earnestly at the monk.

'You are the first person who has seen me as a human being and not as a deformed dwarf. Maybe when I can put money that I have earned myself on the table, my father will forget it for a few minutes too, and be proud of me. That is my dearest wish.'

Don Cristobal laid his hand on Bartolomé's head. 'You will be the best letter-writer in Madrid, and I will do my best to make sure that you get the opportunity to study.'

'You could dictate my first real letter to me,' Bartolomé suggested. 'If you can give me some more paper and ink.'

Accident

IN the meantime, Ana had found Jeronima at the silversmith's. The childish woman came running towards her, howling. The smith had shouted at her when she had tried to put one of the silver chains around her neck.

After Ana had consoled her, they went together to the well. Jeronima offered to carry the basket, but Ana shook her head.

'It's my turn,' she said slyly. 'On the way home, I have to call in to the monastery to pick something up, and then it'll be your turn again to carry the basket.'

They washed the few garments quickly. It didn't occur to Jeronima that there should have been much more washing than these three shirts in such a very heavy basket.

'Will you take me with you again tomorrow?' she asked Ana, as she shouldered the basket.

'Not tomorrow,' said Ana kindly. 'Maybe next week.'

She had decided to ask Don Cristobal to take Bartolomé for only one lesson a week. She was afraid that if she took Jeronima with her too often, someone would smell a rat.

Jeronima refused to wait on her own outside the monastery. 'That bad man will come and shout at me,' she muttered anxiously, pointing an accusing finger over at the silversmith's.

Ana thought it over. She could not bring Jeronima into the monastery. Nobody could be allowed to see Bartolomé.

The church was next to the monastery. Ana led Jeronima into the cool, dim interior of the church. An old woman was sitting in a corner, selling candles. Ana rooted a coin out of her pocket. The candle for Bartolomé's lesson hadn't been paid yet. She pressed the coin into Jeronima's hand.

'Go and buy a candle. Light it over there, in front of the picture. There, where all the candles are burning. I'll be back in a moment.'

Jeronima stared at the old woman. 'Will she shout?' she asked fearfully.

'No,' said Ana calmly. 'Shouting is not allowed in church, and anyway, you can pay for the candle with this coin.'

'I've never paid for anything,' Jeronima confided. 'I'm too stupid for that, my mother says.'

'No, you're not. I think you are clever enough to buy something by yourself.'

'Really?'

'For sure!'

Jeronima went shyly up to the old woman who had a basket of thin white candles beside her. Jeronima turned around a few times to Ana. Every time, Ana nodded encouragingly. Slowly, pride overcame Jeronima's fear. Yes, she *could* buy something herself. When she reached the old woman, she asked confidently for a candle and showed her coin.

Ana made a run for it.

She knocked loudly at the monastery. It took a while before Don Cristobal opened the gate.

'Is Bartolomé ready?' asked Ana hastily, putting down the basket.

Bartolomé came lurching along by the wall.

'Get a move on,' said Ana.

She didn't want Jeronima getting scared and getting into bother again. She hauled her brother roughly into the basket and covered him with the wet washing.

'Is that really necessary?' muttered Don Cristobal. 'Maybe I should just go and speak to your father.'

'No!' cried Bartolomé from inside the basket. 'I can only come if nobody sees me on the street.'

Don Cristobal sighed. What sort of idea did Bartolomé's father have of his son's future as a scribe if he could not show himself in public? Bartolomé certainly was in danger of being mocked, but all this secrecy with the laundry basket was ridiculous. The monk understood that the sister went so far as to wash the clothes that they used to hide Bartolomé's twisted body.

'Can my brother come back next week?' Ana interrupted Don Cristobal's thoughts.

'He can come as often as he likes. I'm always at the gate,' said the monk.

'Tomorrow,' squeaked Bartolomé from his hiding place

'No,' said Ana. 'It will be a week before I can bring you again.'

She opened the gate and dragged the basket out. Don Cristobal noticed that Ana left the laundry basket in front of the entrance and went hurrying off to the church, where a fat woman was waiting for her. She took the woman by the hand and led her to the basket. The woman was smiling at Don Cristobal, but her eyes had an empty, slightly lost look. She bent over willingly as Ana put the straps over her shoulders.

'Now it's my turn again,' said the woman, standing up.

'Goodbye, Don Cristobal,' called Ana.

'Goodbye, Ana. Goodbye, Bartolomé.'

Don Cristobal went back into the monastery. *What a family,* he thought. *Bartolomé crippled, and this young woman without much sense.*

'Did he mean me?' asked Jeronima, when they were out of earshot.

'No. He probably saw someone on the street behind us. That's who he was talking to.'

'But he meant you,' Jeronima insisted.

'Yes,' answered Ana shortly. She was in a hurry. She wanted to get home before her mother came back from the market with Beatríz.

'Will we go to the monastery again the next time?' Jeronima asked.

'Perhaps,' said Ana carefully.

'Then you'll have to tell the monk my name too. I want to be greeted also,' Jeronima demanded.

Ana promised and hurried on.

Jeronima ran after her. 'And can I buy a candle again?' she asked.

'If we get home quickly, you can!'

Jeronima started to walk happily. She overtook Ana. The basket swayed on her broad back. Ana ran behind her.

Too late, Jeronima saw a fabulous coach coming out of a side street. The horses shied when the fat young woman suddenly appeared in front of them. Jeronima's arms flew open with fright. The straps slipped over her round shoulders and the basket fell onto the cobbles with a loud noise. Jeronima ran away, weeping.

The basket swayed, toppled and finally rolled, at first gently, then faster and faster towards the coach. Bartolomé could hear the scrape of wood on the cobbles, the squeak of the wheels, the metallic clang of hoofs on the roadway. He heard the loud voice of the coachman, who was pulling with all his might on the reins. Just as the coach finally pulled up, the laundry basket came to a halt in front of the wheel and broke open.

Bartolomé unwrapped himself from the wet clothes. The newly filled inkpot in his cloth bag had smashed, and Bartolomé's face was all blue. People came running towards him from all directions, staring at him. He couldn't see Ana anywhere. Two footmen in livery jumped down from their place at the back of the coach, trying to keep back the thronging mass of people.

Suddenly Bartolomé heard a girl's voice over his head. He looked up and saw the most charming being he had ever laid eyes on. It was a little girl, a little younger than Beatríz, leaning curiously out of the window of the elegant black coach. Her cheeks were pink with excitement. Her carefully styled blond hair framed her white face with long curls. Some bright yellow flowers were stuck in her hair, behind her left ear. She had big dark eyes and her lips were cherry-red. Bartolomé had never seen such a pretty child. She stuck her arm out of the window and pointed at him.

'Doña,' she called, 'There's something very strange down there.'

The noble lady-in-waiting with a black veil stuck her head out of the window and stared down at Bartolomé. He got frightened and tried to sidle away from the coach and from all these people.

'Doña, it must be a new animal!' called the little girl. 'Look, it walks like a little dog, isn't it funny?' The child clapped her hands in delight. 'I'd like to play with this human dog. Bring it to me,' she said imperiously, as if she was used to getting everything she wanted at once.

'Infanta, it's dirty and it will definitely have fleas,' cried the lady.

'The footmen or the coachman are to catch it,' insisted the Infanta.

Bartolomé had no intention of being caught, and since the people were blocking his way forward, he turned around and tried to creep his way through, under the coach.

If only Ana were here, thought Bartolomé. Why didn't she come and rescue him?

Ana was pressing herself up against the wall of a house. Rigid with shock, she watched the drama. At first she thought that the basket, together with Bartolomé, would be squashed under the hooves of the horses or the wheels of the coach. She breathed a sigh of relief when she saw that Bartolomé seemed to be unharmed. Then she saw the pretty child looking delightedly out of the window of the coach.

It must be the little Infanta Margarita, thought Ana. What other child in Madrid was driven in a carriage accompanied by footmen? Her father had often told them about the pretty princess. Her father! Ana looked in horror towards the coach. There he sat, ramrod straight, staring down at Bartolomé. What would he do with Bartolomé, and with her, if he caught sight of her?

Juan was doing nothing, apart from wishing the ground would open and swallow him up. His own crippled son, whom he believed to be holed up in the back room of the apartment, had stopped the royal coach in full view of everyone. Worse still, he had attracted the attention of the Infanta. Juan sat on the coachman's seat as if he were nailed to it, but he was seized with a dreadful anger. How dare Bartolomé turn up here and confront him like this! He felt horribly humiliated. Now everyone would see what kind of monster he had for a son.

'I want him!' The words of the Infanta pressed in on Juan and broke his torpor. He leapt down from his seat, grabbed Bartolomé by the foot and dragged him out from under the coach. He would dearly like to have thrown Bartolomé at the wall of a nearby house, over the heads of all these staring people.

'Coachman, give me the human dog!' The Infanta made to open the door of the coach but her lady-in-waiting held her back.

'Infanta,' she said, 'I'm sure he stinks and has lice.'

She looked with revulsion at Bartolomé, who was being held upside down by the ankle by his father.

I don't stink, thought Bartolomé. He wished his father would defend him. But Juan said nothing. He looked at Bartolomé as if he were a total stranger.

In spite of her fear of her father, Ana had pushed her way to him through the onlookers. She didn't want to abandon Bartolomé.

Bartolomé saw her and stretched out his hands to her.

'*He* can wash him, then, and then bring him to me,' insisted the Infanta.

'Certainly!' Juan bowed, and as he stood up straight again, he caught sight of Ana. He pushed Bartolomé into her arms.

Bartolomé clung to Ana. She held him tight. The two of them could sense the violent anger that radiated from Juan. Ana tried to protect Bartolomé from it with her embrace.

'Who's that?' asked the Infanta jealously.

'My daughter Ana, Infanta. She'll wash him.'

The Infanta nodded her agreement. 'But I want to have him afterwards. He's going to be my human dog.' She leant back happily.

'Go home, disappear,' Juan ordered his two children quietly. Ana didn't hesitate for a moment. With Bartolomé in her arms, she hurried away.

Home Again

ANA carried the weeping Bartolomé home through the streets. Bartolomé hid his face in her blouse, as if that would prevent people from seeing his deformed body. But he could not close his ears. He could hear the cornerboys shouting insults after him. Someone tried to trip Ana up. She stumbled but did not fall.

They arrived home at last, in an awful state. Upstairs in the living room Ana let Bartolomé slip to the floor. Manuel started to roar with fright when he saw Bartolomé's inky blue face. Beatríz stared curiously at her older brother and sister.

'How come Bartolomé was out even though Papa doesn't allow that?' she asked. 'If I tell Papa ...' she murmured to herself.

'Keep quiet,' Isabel scolded. Something bad had happened and the last person she wanted to think about at that moment was Juan.

Offended, Beatríz pulled a face. She was not stupid. She had long been aware that there was a secret between her mother and the older children. She'd been sent out on the flimsiest of excuses too often lately and she'd noticed that conversations came to a sudden halt when she came into the apartment. She'd felt left out. Now she was delighted. Ana and Bartolomé were sure to be punished.

'What have you done to him?' Isabel took hold of Ana by the arms and shook her hard. 'Did you go to Don Cristobal?'

'I'm so sorry. I'm so sorry,' Ana kept stammering. She broke free and ran into the bedroom.

'Bartolomé, what happened?' Isabel hunkered down in front of her son, angry but worried at the same time.

'I don't want to go. She can't have me!' cried Bartolomé tearfully.

'Who?'

'The girl from the coach,' said Bartolomé.

A coach? That reminded her of Juan. He'd be home soon. She must have Bartolomé washed by then. She emptied a water jug into a large basin.

'Take this jug and get more water,' she ordered Beatríz.

'I've already been to the well today,' moaned Beatríz. 'There's enough water.' She wanted to be there when her father came home from work.

Isabel gave her a clip on the ear. Wailing, Beatríz took the empty jug and ran angrily out. If they tried to pull the wool over her father's eyes, she'd tell all, she decided.

Bartolomé used his hands and feet to try to beat off the wet facecloth.

'No washing,' he roared, and, when she ignored him, he bit despairingly into Isabel's arm. He had gone too far now. Since Bartolomé had learnt to read, Isabel had never smacked him. But now she gave her dwarf son a thrashing like never before. She hit him wildly about the legs, the crooked back, the head. When Bartolomé tried to protect himself with his arms, she beat him even harder. She should never have been party to all these secrets.

'So I shouldn't bother about you?' she yelled angrily. 'Well stay as you are, then, and just wait till your father gets home. He can do what he likes with you.'

She threw him in to Ana in the little bedroom and banged the door on them. Her shoulders were shaking.

Isabel saw Manuel cowering in terror in the corner. She went to him to console him with a hug. Manuel squealed. Was she going to beat him too and lock him in the little room? He fled down the stairs and threw himself at Doña Rosita's door. He would feel safe in her arms.

Isabel sank into an armchair and started to cry. What would Juan do to her and the children when he came home?

Just as Doña Rosita opened the door and took the distraught Manuel up in her arms, Juan entered the house. He took no notice of his little son and the neighbour woman. The Infanta had sent him to get the cleaned-up human dog immediately. She didn't want to wait until the next day. Juan was furious. He would never have believed that his own children could have upset him so badly. And whatever Isabel had to say, he was no longer willing to protect Bartolomé. He could find out for himself what it was like to be the butt of mockery for everyone. And Ana? He could not throw her out. In spite of his towering rage, he was not equal to that. But he would beat her so badly that she would never again challenge him.

He rushed up the stairs. When he fled from the apartment, Manuel had left the door open. As Juan went in the door upstairs, Doña Rosita took a basket and left the house quickly, with Manuel in her arms. Whatever was going to happen upstairs, she didn't want to hear it.

Juan stood in the middle of the room. Isabel's soft weeping and the sobs of his children, muffled by the bedroom door, did nothing to diminish his anger. On the contrary, it drove him into an even worse rage.

'Please don't do anything to them,' stammered Isabel, when she became aware of Juan's presence.

Juan walked past her, yanked the door open and hauled Ana up from her sleeping mat. He hit her with his bare fist. The blows hit her on the arms, with which she tried to protect her face. Then Juan grabbed his daughter's slender wrist with one hand, and with the other, he punched her repeatedly in the face. It wasn't until it had swollen up and blood dropped from her nose that he became aware of Isabel's distraught voice.

'You'll kill her. You'll kill her. Stop!'

At that, Juan let the girl fall to the floor. He turned around to Isabel.

'Did you know about this too?' he asked. His voice had suddenly gone quiet.

'Me?' The fear Isabel felt was written in her eyes. 'I wanted to tell you, but it ...'

'You knew!' Juan shook his head. He could understand nothing any more.

'We wanted to surprise you,' whispered Isabel hoarsely.

Juan landed a mighty punch on Isabel's temple. She let out a loud cry, swayed and crumpled to the ground.

Bartolomé knew it was his turn next. His father's anger would definitely be even worse against him. He closed his eyes. There was no one to save him. But Juan did not hit him. Instead, he dragged his son into the front room to the washbasin. When Bartolomé opened his eyes, he saw the reflection of his blue face in the water. It reminded him of Don Matteo drowning kittens in a bucket back in the village.

'Papa, please don't!' he stuttered.

Juan pulled off Bartolomé's clothes with shaking hands.

He had great difficulty in controlling himself. Then he washed Bartolomé's naked, crooked body carefully. His movements were firm but not rough. Bartolomé hung there in his arms, limp as a ragdoll.

The thought ran through Bartolomé's head: *He's only doing nothing to me because he's going to take me to the Infanta.* He wished he'd been beaten like Ana and his mother. He wanted to have bruises and welts. Any pain would be better than this empty realisation that his father was going to deliver him to the royal court like a lifeless or, worse, an unloved, unvalued commodity.

Parting

ISABEL had crawled to Ana. They cowered silently together at the doorway into the back bedroom and watched Juan's movements with fearful eyes. Juan looked over to them, when he had finished cleaning Bartolomé up. He had even washed Bartolomé's tousled hair with soap until it stood up fluffily on his head.

'Bring me his best shirt and trousers,' Juan told Isabel. Isabel looked at him uncomprehendingly. 'Do it! I have no time. We are expected.'

'No,' whispered Ana to Isabel. 'He can't do this.'

'What's going on with Bartolomé? Where are you taking him?' Isabel dared to ask.

Juan laughed a loud, ugly laugh. 'He's going to have a fine time. The Infanta of Spain wants him as a plaything.'

'Plaything!?'

'He's going to be her little human dog. He'll go scuttling after balls and lap up milk from a silver salver,' Juan explained in a hard voice.

Ana started to cry again.

'You can't allow it!' Isabel shrieked at her husband.

'Who am I to prevent it? The Infanta has seen him and now she wants him.'

'You are his father. You have to help him, protect him.'

'He broke his promise, so why should I protect him any more?'

'He is a *child*, Juan. He is your *son*.'

'I do not have a son who is a human dog,' said Juan. There was a finality about his tone and it was clear that he would not tolerate any more opposition.

Since Isabel did not budge, Juan himself went and got Bartolomé's best clothes and dressed him. Bartolomé put up no struggle. There was no point. Not even his mother could see a way to help him. And his father?

I never had a proper father, thought Bartolomé bitterly. This man had barely put up with him, never loved him.

'You'll have to say goodbye now,' said Juan. He stepped back and turned away.

Isabel hesitated. Bartolomé was sitting on the floor beside the table. He did not look up. His head, pushed forward by the hump, almost touched his short legs. Like a grotesque dwarf in a puppet theatre whose strings had been cut, he sat there, saying nothing.

Isabel knelt down in front of him and embraced his crooked body. She kissed his head, his neck, his hump. But she couldn't look into his face. That would break her heart.

Ana came too, but she did not dare to hug him. She was too afraid of another outburst from her father if she dirtied Bartolomé's clean clothes with her bloody face. She put her hand on his hair, but did not stroke it. Then she ran back into the little room.

'That'll do,' said Juan at last. He lifted Bartolomé out of the arms of his mother and carried him out of the apartment, down the stairs, through the streets to the great royal palace of Alcázar.

A little later, Beatríz came back with the water jug. She had dawdled at the well and wandered home, coming the long way round. Her desire to see Ana and Bartolomé being punished had been replaced by anxiety. As she climbed up the dark stairs, the silence behind the door of the apartment was uncanny. She waited for a while uncertainly on the landing and listened. Not a sound, not a movement broke the ghostly silence.

Carefully, she opened the door. Her mother was sitting at the table in the main room, still as a statue. Her hands lay idly on the table top. At the window stood Ana, her swollen face lit by the sun. Beatríz had never before seen how blows could disfigure a face. She almost let the jug fall from her hands. She looked around. How much worse must Bartolomé have been punished! The door to the bedroom was open. Beatríz looked in. The little room was empty.

'Where is Bartolomé?' she asked in a small voice.

'Gone,' answered Isabel.

'But he'll be back?'

Isabel shook her head. 'No, never again.'

Beatríz had never cared much for Bartolomé. In the village, she'd even been a bit ashamed of him, and she'd avoided playing near him when he sat out on the village square. But he couldn't just disappear out of her life like that.

'Is he dead?' she asked. She thought it was possible that her father's anger could have been that terrible. When she saw Ana's face, she could not believe that Bartolomé's little body could withstand such a beating.

'No, Papa had to take him to the royal palace. The Infanta wants to play with him,' said Isabel.

Beatríz's eyes widened. She stared open-mouthed at her

mother. How come Bartolomé had not been punished? How come he was actually rewarded for the bad thing he had done? Why did the Infanta want to have a crippled child, of all people, as a playmate? Jealousy welled up in her.

'How come Papa didn't take me too? I'd love to play with a real princess.' Her disappointment was written all over her face. In her head, her father had come home in order to find a playmate for the little princess, and because she herself was not there, he had taken Bartolomé instead.

'Oh, Beatríz,' said Isabel standing up. She opened her arms and the little girl ran into them, weeping.

'Believe me,' whispered Isabel to her, 'Bartolomé didn't want to go, but he had to.'

'Then he's a silly billy,' said Beatríz.

Isabel kissed her. She didn't have the heart to explain to Beatríz what it meant to have to be the plaything of the spoilt princess.

'Mama, the next time the Infanta wants someone to play with, Papa must take me,' Beatríz pleaded.

Isabel sensed that Ana wanted to say something. She shook her head. Beatríz was too small. She wouldn't understand.

'Mama, does Bartolomé really have to stay there for ever?' Beatríz had just remembered what her mother had said at the start.

Isabel nodded. 'Princesses are like that,' she said.

Beatríz thought for a moment. 'I think,' she said at last, 'I'd rather not play with a princess after all.'

Part 2

Alcázar

JUAN carried Bartolomé silently through the streets of Madrid to the enormous walls of Alcázar.

Hundreds of people lived and worked in the palace, from the lowest kitchen maid to the mighty ministers of the Council of State. The court of Philip the Fourth, King of Spain and lord of numerous colonies, was a world in itself. Anyone who managed to gain the favour of the king could make a career even as a simple citizen. However, anyone on whom his wrath fell lost, in short order, all his privileges and offices, and if he did not leg it fast out of the orbit of the court with all its intrigue, calumny and corruption, could easily end up a beggar on the streets of Madrid. Juan knew that things went on behind the gorgeous façades of Alcázar that would have horrified an honest, hardworking citizen.

Anyone who had the slightest influence was liable, before long, to try to supplement his earnings, which were often irregularly paid. Juan himself had to hand over some of his pay packet to the chief stablemaster. It never crossed his mind to complain about it; that was just how things were. In any case, there was no way he could complain even if he had wanted to. Protocol was strict. The coachmen were under the chief stablemaster, and it was unthinkable for Juan to lay his case before a more senior person.

Juan hurried as fast as he could through the silent courtyards of Alcázar. He hoped he would not meet anyone he knew, who might ask questions.

When he finally reached the gate to the Quarto del Principe, that part of the palace in which the royal family lived, he handed Bartolomé over to one of the sentries.

'He's for the Infanta,' said Juan.

'Papa,' whispered Bartolomé, feeling the stranger's arms reaching for him. 'Papa, when are you going to take me home again?'

Juan turned wordlessly and hurried away. Bartolomé looked after him as he went over the cobbled yard and under the arch of a gateway and disappeared out of Bartolomé's life. The sentry looked with revulsion at the humped dwarf in his arms. At least he didn't stink and was neatly if poorly dressed. *It's a whim of the rich*, he thought, *to keep such creatures for their amusement.*

He knocked at the gate. 'For the Infanta of Spain,' announced the soldier.

And so Bartolomé was passed like a parcel from person to person, through countless corridors and rooms with thick carpets and richly coloured tapestries and paintings. At last, he was carried by one of the guard of honour to the chamberlain of the Infanta, who passed him to the first lady-in-waiting, Doña Marcela de Ulloa.

'Here he is,' she said crossly.

Bartolomé recognised her. It was the woman dressed in black from the coach. Doña Marcela de Ulloa had been in charge of the little court that had surrounded the royal child from birth. At the age of five, Infanta Margarita had at her disposal six pages – sons of noble families – three aristocratic ladies-in-waiting, a priest and a confessor, two doctors and a surgeon, a teacher, a tutor, a dancing and music master, four chamberlains, a guard of honour consisting of twenty soldiers, ten footmen, two chambermaids, five lower serving women, a baker and a confectioner, three cooks with their kitchen staffs, two water carriers and five washerwomen. Doña Marcela de Ulloa was in charge of all these people, and she alone decided who should be admitted to the Infanta's presence.

Doña de Ulloa considered to whom she should pass on this dwarf, so that he could be appropriately dressed and instructed. Her choice fell on Doña Maria Augustina de Sarmiento, the youngest lady-in-waiting. She enjoyed looking after Infanta Margarita's menagerie of animals and dwarves. She never missed an opportunity to entertain the princess with these creatures.

'Fetch Maria Augustina,' Doña de Ulloa ordered a page standing next to her, staring the whole time at Bartolomé, who was sitting on the floor. The page bowed and hurried off.

Doña de Ulloa turned to Bartolomé. She was never sure how much these deformed creatures understood. All the same, it was necessary to make sure they took in the most important rules of behaviour at court.

'You are not to speak unless someone asks you a question. If you have to answer, you are to call the Infanta "Your Highness". And you are not to look her in the eye and you're to speak only briefly. Nobody may turn their back on the Infanta of Spain. Anything she asks, you are to do immediately. You may not laugh, shout or cry. Somebody will be in charge of you, to supervise you, and, since you seem not to be able to walk yourself, to make sure you are carried anywhere you are required.'

115

Bartolomé let this torrent of words wash over him without saying a word himself. Doña de Ulloa got cross with the dwarf. She didn't notice how upset Bartolomé was. In her view, he was awkward or stupid or both.

'Do you have any idea what an honour it is to have attracted the interest of the Infanta?' she rebuked him. 'She rescued you from the gutter. For that, you owe her infinite gratitude. And the best way to show that is to fulfil her every wish. Then it will go well with you. Understood?'

Bartolomé nodded helplessly. He had been handed over to these people, but not pulled out of the gutter. He had a mother and brothers and sisters. He had Don Cristobal. But they were out of his reach and could not come to his aid.

'Well, then,' said Doña de Ulloa contentedly.

'Madam?' Maria Augustina de Sarmiento curtsied to the first lady-in-waiting. She was a young girl with a pretty, open face.

She looked curiously at Bartolomé. Until now, she'd considered Marie Barbola, a fat dwarf with a bloated round face, the ugliest creature in the Infanta's menagerie. But this little fellow outdid her.

'It's the human doggy that the Infanta spotted on her outing. She wants to play with him. You'll dress him appropriately, and when the princess does not want him around, then the dwarf Marie Barbola is to look after him,' Doña de Ulloa ordered.

A human dog! Indeed, this dwarf with his short legs, his hump and his long arms was more like an animal than a human. The Infanta had never owned anything like this. Maria Augustina had a lively imagination. She was already thinking about the best way to dress the creature so that it really did resemble a dog.

'I need bathwater and seamstresses, and they are to bring me brown, furry material,' she announced confidently.

Doña de Ulloa nodded her agreement. She had made a good choice. Maria Augustina was the right person to dress up this dwarf.

'You can take him away and order anything you need,' the first lady-in-waiting said graciously.

'Follow me,' Maria Augustina said to Bartolomé.

'He can't walk, only crawl,' said Doña de Ulloa. 'You'll have to carry him.'

I can walk if someone holds my hand, Bartolomé wanted to say, looking up into the lovely face of Maria Augustina. He trusted her, and would have liked to take her by the hand. So he stuck out his long arm freely to the lady-in-waiting. Maria Augustina pulled back in horror.

'You can't expect me to do that. Marie Barbola can bring him to my room,' she said in disgust. She lifted her skirts and, after a quick curtsy, she hurried away. She would never carry one of these creatures.

Bright red and deeply wounded, Bartolomé hung back. A little later, he was grabbed roughly by a dwarf woman.

'Come with me. Give me your hand. I'm not going to carry you,' said the dwarf that had to be Marie Barbola.

Although she was not much taller than Bartolomé, she was astonishingly strong. With a practised hand, she supported him so that he could totter along beside her.

'What's your name?' she asked when they were out of earshot of the first lady-in-waiting.

'Bartolomé,' answered Bartolomé softly.

'Lovely name. But nobody will call you that here. The Infanta likes to think up names for her playthings. She calls me

Moonface, when she's in good humour. Cowpat, when she's in a bad mood.'

'I'm not a toy,' Bartolomé dared to contradict her. 'I am a child, and I want to go home.'

Marie Barbola laughed bitterly. 'From now on, you are her toy and the palace is your home. The quicker you get used to that, the better. Make sure that she likes you and it will be fine. She'll give you sweets, and you'll be allowed to go everywhere with her. But woe betide you if you annoy her. Then you'll be thrown into a corner like a broken old doll.'

'When she doesn't want me any more, can I go home then?' asked Bartolomé hopefully.

Marie Barbola gave him a slap in the face with her free hand. 'Don't even think about it.' But when she saw Bartolomé's terrified face, she stopped in the long corridor and turned to him with a serious face. 'If the Infanta wants rid of you, you will be thrown out into the gutter in front of the palace. Nobody will bother to take you home.'

Bartolomé's cheeks were burning.

'You're lucky that Maria Augustina has taken you on,' Marie Barbola informed him. 'Her pretty little head is full of ideas. I've been here for years. But only since she's had to look after me has the Infanta started to take any notice of me. Recently, Maria Augustina had my face painted yellow. Then a servant had to hang me upside down, from a rope, in front of the Infanta's bedroom window, moving me back and forward. The princess was thrilled. Now she calls me Moonface and she's given me a new dress.'

'She called me Human Dog when I was lying in front of her coach,' murmured Bartolomé.

Marie Barbola clapped delightedly. 'It's good if she has a name for you already. I'm sure Maria Augustina will think of something good. We'll go to her at once. She doesn't like waiting and we'd better not annoy her.'

A Human Dog

WHEN Marie Barbola propelled Bartolomé into Maria Augustina's room, several people were already waiting for them. Two servants had charge of a wooden bathtub. Three water carriers were filling it with warm water. Maria Augustina emptied a phial of bath oil into it with her own hand. It smelt of the Infanta's favourite perfume.

Two seamstresses and an assistant were all set in one part of the room. The assistant, a thin girl barely ten years old, was struggling to hold heavy bales of material in her arms. Two page-boys were chatting idly near the window. As the serving girl started to undress Bartolomé they came closer and stared without embarrassment at his back where the bones were visible under the skin and had grown into a hump. They laughed.

Bartolomé was put into the water, even though his father had already washed him, and was scrubbed. He didn't have the nerve to protest. Afterwards, the serving girl rubbed him dry with a big towel. But as she reached for Bartolomé's shirt, Maria Augustina shook her head. 'He's going to have a new outfit.'

The serving girl bundled up his few pieces of clothing and left the room. The manservants carried the bathtub out.

'The Infanta wants a human dog,' said Maria Augustina. 'Therefore he'll have a costume made of brown material which will envelop him from head to toe. Only his face can remain visible.'

The seamstresses nodded eagerly and pulled Bartolomé out of the towel, into which he had crept in order to avoid the gaping of the pages.

The older woman measured his body. Meanwhile, Maria Augustina chose a material. She decided on a bolt of soft, dark brown velvet.

'We have no time to lose,' she said. 'I want to surprise the Infanta with it this evening at bedtime.'

The women cut out the material on a table in the corner of the room, and got to work. Bartolomé had wrapped himself up again in the towel as soon as they had left him in peace. He sat quietly in the middle of the room and waited. Maria Augustina disappeared, followed by the pages and the dwarf woman. For two hours Bartolomé sat on the floor, watching the seamstresses sewing away, seam by seam. The assistant threaded needles and laid pieces of material side by side, and, when she had time, she stared over at Bartolomé as if he was the strangest thing she had ever seen.

Late in the afternoon, Maria Augustina came back with her retinue. She bent over Bartolomé, raised his head up and looked into his face.

'It is far too pale,' she said accusingly. 'As a brown dog, you'll need a dark face. We'll have to paint you.'

She straightened up and beckoned a page.

'Go to Master Velázquez in the studio and request an apprentice who will bring me a selection of brown paints,' she demanded.

The apprentice painter was a young lad in a paint-spattered smock. He brought a little box and laid it in front of Bartolomé on the floor. He looked curiously at Bartolomé, who stared anxiously at the box.

'It's only got paints and paintbrushes in it, no instruments of torture,' the apprentice whispered and gave a wink. He lifted the lid. Bartolomé bent forward a little and looked in. He saw a row of little bottles.

The apprentice turned up the lid of the box and set the bottles on it. They were labelled on the outside, and they contained powders of every shade of brown. *Umber, burnt umber, Cassel earth, bitumen, sepia, Siena, burnt Siena, ochre ...* Bartolomé read. He hadn't known that there were so many kinds of brown. Sepia was so dark that it seemed almost black, whereas Siena was a reddish brown. Umber was like dark, freshly ploughed earth, and burnt umber was the same colour as the clay oven at home.

Next to these stood bottles of clear fluids. Bartolomé murmured the strange-sounding names: linseed oil, spirit gum, Venetian turpentine, poppy-seed oil, tragacanth, distilled water.

The apprentice painter was still taking items out of the box. A marble bowl, a flat clay dish, a thick white sheet of glass, a pestle and several little spoons. The last thing he laid on the lid was a single hen's egg. He looked around.

'I'm all set,' he said to the page who was standing next to him.

'I'll just see if Doña de Sarmiento can make time for you,' replied the page from on high.

'He'll choke on his own arrogance,' murmured the apprentice, as the page strolled, with a rolling gait, to Maria Augustina, who was supervising the work of the seamstresses. Bartolomé laughed involuntarily. He put his hand quickly in front of his mouth. Laughing was sure to be forbidden. The apprentice painter gave him a surprised look. Then he grinned.

'Don't you agree?' he whispered and imitated the page's snooty expression. Bartolomé bit his hand to prevent himself from bursting out with loud laughter. His crooked body was shaking.

'I'm Andrés. What are they planning to do with you?' asked the apprentice.

'Bartolomé,' whispered Bartolomé. 'They are going to make me a human dog for the Infanta.'

Andrés seemed shocked. He had often had to help out with plans of the ladies-in-waiting. For example, once they had wanted to paint a pony for the Infanta with black and white stripes, to turn it into an African animal of some sort. He had painted cats purple and once he'd had to tint the hair of all the pages green. He'd had to paint the doughy face of Marie Barbola yellow recently to make a full moon of it. He hadn't realised that she wasn't going to take part in a play, but was going to be hung upside down from a rope in front of a window. When they had told him that, he felt guilty.

'A dog?' asked Andrés.

'I don't want to,' said Bartolomé. 'I'm a human being.'

Andrés nodded. But what could he do? He could do nothing to stop it. He was only a little insignificant apprentice who was lucky enough to be trained by the king's court painter.

'Did you know that a painter always paints a dog into his picture when he wants to represent courage and loyalty?' he said, trying to console Bartolomé.

'Really?'

'If the lady-in-waiting asks me to make you up like a dog, I will paint you so that you look like the bravest dog in all of Spain,' he promised.

'Why is there chatter going on here?' complained Maria Augustina, appearing out of nowhere.

Quickly, she chose two colours. 'Dark brown for the snout and a light brown for the rest of the face.' She was pointing at the umber and the ochre.

Bartolomé watched Andrés shaking a little of the coarse ochre powder onto the glass platter and grinding it with the pestle. Then he mixed linseed oil with tragacanth and a trace of distilled water in the marble bowl. Then, to Bartolomé's surprise, he cracked the egg into the flat clay dish and beat it with a spoon until the yolk and the white formed a foam. He poured part of this into the marble bowl. He stirred it carefully with the spoon and then shook the finely ground ochre powder into it until it became a gleaming light brown paste.

Bartolomé watched what he did. He hadn't known that this was how you made paint, though his mother had sometimes boiled onion skins to make a brew that would dye wool a reddish colour.

Andrés noticed how interested Bartolomé was, and he felt flattered by the attention. In the studio, he was the youngest, the dogsbody. He was not paid much heed, either by the master painter or by the other apprentices. He was entrusted with only the lowliest tasks.

Andrés sat down on the floor in front of Bartolomé and dipped a thin paintbrush with a short head into the paint. Carefully, he painted Bartolomé's face.

'Close your eyes so you don't get paint in them,' he said to the dwarf, who was still wrapped in the towel. Bartolomé felt the paintbrush brushing softly over his closed eyelids. It tickled, and he grimaced.

'It'll be over in a minute,' murmured Andrés kindly.

When he had painted most of Bartolomé's face light brown, he asked for clean water and fresh cloths. He rinsed the paintbrush carefully and cleaned the glass sheet, the pestle, spoon and bowl.

Andrés noticed how Bartolomé watched all his movements carefully. 'Would you like to try it for yourself?' he offered.

'Could I really?' asked Bartolomé, surprised.

Andrés nodded. He was glad to see how Bartolomé's sad eyes suddenly lit up. Like a master craftsman, Andrés instructed his pupil and he was amazed how neatly Bartolomé crushed the umber powder on the glass platter and mixed it with the linseed oil, tragacanth, water and the rest of the egg to make a paste. At first, the spoon just made dark streaks, but soon the pigment jelled into a uniform dark brown emulsion.

'I have made proper paint, all by myself,' breathed Bartolomé, overcome, and it didn't bother him at all that Andrés smeared the dark brown paste in a thick layer over his mouth and nose.

Maria Augustina came back and regarded Bartolomé's painted face critically.

'It'll be fine with the costume,' she said at last.

Andrés cleaned his utensils and bottles and packed them back into the box. As he closed it over, he waved goodbye to Bartolomé.

'Thank you, Andrés,' said Bartolomé softly.

Andrés was taken aback. He hadn't expected the sad little creature to thank him. He was pleased, and at the same time he felt ashamed. Who knew what sort of tricks they would play on the dwarf.

'Bartolomé.' Andrés bent down, close to the grotesquely painted face with its grateful eyes. 'Never forget that you are the bravest dog in all of Spain!'

Dog-training

HOW am I supposed to feel like the bravest dog in Spain? thought Bartolomé as Marie Barbola put the dog costume on him. The worst part was to see his hands, the only parts of him that had grown properly, disappearing into the fabric 'paws' of the costume. When Marie Barbola had fastened the buttons on his stomach, Bartolomé had to crawl to the big mirror, dragging a long tail behind him. The pealing laughter of the pages followed him. He hardly dared to look in the mirror. When at last he did so, he saw a little brown hump-backed dog with floppy ears, which had been sewn on either side of the costume's headpiece and which dangled back and forth. Bartolomé looked unhappily at his reflection. No way could he be a brave dog.

'Marie Barbola, you'll have to teach him to bark and do tricks!' Maria Augustina instructed.

The pages clapped ecstatically. One of them gave a cheeky pull on Bartolomé's long tail. The other lifted up one of the floppy ears and roared into it, 'Bark!'

Brave dogs don't bark, thought Bartolomé. *Brave dogs bite when people annoy them.* But he knew he wouldn't be allowed to do that.

Bartolomé had to creep on all fours behind Marie Barbola through the corridors of the palace kitchen wing. There the dwarf woman had a tiny, sparsely furnished room with a

126

discarded sofa that served as a bed, a chest, a table with a cracked washbasin and a battered tin jug. There was a worn carpet on the floor and a little stove provided heat in winter. The single window looked out onto a minuscule inner courtyard that let light into other rooms.

Marie Barbola climbed up on the sofa. 'Are you hungry?' she asked Bartolomé.

'Yes.'

At lunch, he'd been so excited about going to see Don Cristobal again that he'd hardly been able to get anything down, and since then he'd had nothing to eat.

Marie Barbola slipped down from the sofa and disappeared. She came back shortly with a bowl, in which steamed chunks of bread that had been fried in olive oil.

Bartolomé's stomach rumbled loudly. Marie Barbola gave an amused giggle and put the bowl beside her on the sofa.

'If you bark, you'll get a piece.'

Bartolomé let out a strangled gurgle. Why did even this dwarf woman have to tease him?

'That sounded like a whimper, Bartolomé,' she said encouragingly and threw him a piece of bread.

Bartolomé tried clumsily to pick it up in his paw.

'No!' Marie Barbola admonished him. 'That's not how a dog eats. Behave yourself, or I'll eat it all up on you.'

She stuck a piece of bread greedily into her mouth. Humiliated, Bartolomé crouched over the food and caught it in his teeth. He chewed and swallowed. It tasted of nothing.

'Well done!' she praised him. 'And now bark!'

Bartolomé barked and stood up and begged. Each time he did it to Marie Barbola's satisfaction, he was thrown a piece of bread.

Hunger and the knowledge that he had no other choice drove him to play along with this grisly game.

'You really are a regular dog,' Marie Barbola snorted as she made Bartolomé raise his hind leg at the leg of the table.

He could manage to hold this pose unsteadily for a moment, but then he fell over. Marie Barbola threw him the last piece of bread. Bartolomé ignored it.

'I don't want to be a dog!' he wailed in despair.

Marie Barbola shrugged her shoulders. The dwarf should know by now that he had no alternative.

'El Primo. He's like me. Why can't I be a secretary?' Bartolomé pleaded. 'I can read and write.'

Marie Barbola laughed bitterly. Everyone knew El Primo. He was one lucky fellow.

'The Infanta wants you as a human dog. It doesn't matter, Bartolomé, who you are or what you can do. You have to be what she wants,' she told him in no uncertain terms. 'And you needn't start getting uppity. Reading and writing are of no interest to anyone. That'll make you nothing but enemies.'

Bartolomé hung his head and bit his lip. He mustn't cry. That would ruin his make-up.

'It's only a game,' said Marie Barbola, suddenly kind. 'A game that rich folks play. Don't take it to heart. If you're smart, and steer clear of intrigues and gossip, you can have a wonderful life at court. Think of it as a stage play, with you in the leading role.'

A game. A play. Bartolomé sighed.

'You'll see, you'll have plenty of time for being human later. I'm sure the Infanta won't want to have you around the whole time,' Marie Barbola said confidently.

The Infanta

INFANTA MARGARITA was five years old, and even though she was surrounded by gorgeous things and dressed in the most costly clothes, she was, at the end of the day, just a spoilt, lonely little girl. She hardly ever saw her parents, King Philip the Fourth of Spain and Queen Ana. Her half-sister, Maria Teresa, at sixteen, had long outgrown the nursery.

Sometimes specially selected noble children were invited to play. But they were so intimidated by their parents' exhortations to good behaviour that they just stood stiffly around and did everything that Margarita asked of them. In any case, running wild and tumbling about the place was impossible in the fancy outfits they wore, all decked out in ruffles and lace. If any of the children did the slightest thing to annoy Margarita, he or she was borne off immediately by one of the mothers that hung around or one of the ladies-in-waiting. Nobody was allowed to cross the little Infanta of Spain.

Margarita got bored with this kind of company, and the only real friends she had were animals, dwarves and deformed people. With these creatures, she was able to enjoy life. The animals were housed in a pretty little stable building, while the human curiosities were accommodated in the palace and were always available to her as playthings.

Among them was José, whose flexible body seemed to

contain no bones. He entertained the little princess by twisting his body into every conceivable shape. Nono was a totally spherical dwarf who could roll like a ball. Maria Augustina de Sarmiento, who was the most creative lady-in-waiting, had invented an amusing game of skittles, whereby pages were made to stand around in the corridors, stiff as ninepins, and Margarita tried to knock them down with Nono. The thing Margarita liked best, however, were the spooky stories that were told by Marie Barbola, the dwarf with the expressionless moonface.

'Where is Marie Barbola? She should be here with me!' the Infanta demanded after supper, when her little royal household withdrew and she was left to her own devices. She knew that it was bedtime, but she wanted to drag it out a bit.

'She is preparing a surprise for the princess.'

Margarita pulled a face and stamped her foot. 'I don't want a surprise. She is to come here immediately!'

'But, but!' Doña de Ulloa chipped in. 'A Spanish Infanta always keeps her cool.'

Doña de Ulloa was the only one who occasionally chided Margarita gently.

Margarita's pretty face flushed red. 'Nobody ever refuses the Spanish Infanta anything!' she cried.

Doña de Ulloa took this in her stride. Even if she didn't show it externally, she always thought of the Infanta as just a little girl. She always spoke respectfully, but she did not tolerate opposition, not even from the Infanta.

'As far as I am aware, the Infanta herself has expressed a wish for this surprise,' she said to the cross little girl.

Margarita thought this over. What surprise had she asked for? She couldn't remember, but her curiosity was aroused.

'Doña de Ulloa, what did I say I wanted?' she wheedled.

'Has the wish of the Infanta, which she expressed so fervently when she was out in her coach today, become so unimportant that she has already forgotten it?'

Out in her carriage! The extraordinary little creature that had scuttled out in front of the wheels of the coach! Margarita jumped with joy.

'My human doggy!' she cried. 'I want to see it and play with it. Bring it immediately to my bedroom.'

Doña de Ulloa coughed politely. Margarita looked at her for a moment in astonishment. Then she got it. She gave a perfect curtsy and asked nicely: 'Please may the human dog be brought?'

Doña de Ulloa nodded contentedly. 'When the princess has put on her nightdress, the human dog can be brought,' she announced calmly.

'Quickly, please,' cried Margarita impatiently.

Maria Augustina hurried away. Hopefully Marie Barbola had completed the training by now.

The dwarf woman and Bartolomé were sitting together in the little room on the sofa. Bartolomé had laid his great head in Marie Barbola's lap, and, exhausted, had nodded off. She was stroking him contentedly. Bartolomé was able to bark properly now, and perform tricks, and he had promised her not to disappoint the Infanta.

As the door flew open and Maria Augustina entered the bare little room, Bartolomé shot upright.

'What's going on here?' cried the lady-in-waiting. 'A dog does not sit on the sofa.'

Marie Barbola shooed Bartolomé away and he crept into a corner.

'Can he bark and beg?' Maria Augustina asked.

The dwarf woman nodded. 'Bark!' she commanded. 'Do what I taught you to do.'

Bartolomé closed his eyes briefly and tried to see himself as the bravest dog in Spain, or at least to feel like an actor playing an important part. Then he gave a good loud bark.

'And now the tricks,' ordered Marie Barbola.

Bartolomé sat up and begged, bared his teeth, pretended to slurp something up off the floor, fetched a little ball that the dwarf threw for him and finished by raising his leg.

Maria Augustina roared with laughter when this made Bartolomé lose his balance and tumble to the floor.

'Wonderful!' she declared.

Marie Barbola beamed with pride. She was hoping she'd be allowed to go with them. The Infanta would be sure to reward her with a little attention.

Maria Augustina pulled a gold-embroidered leather collar and a lead out of the pocket of her dress and gave them to the dwarf woman.

'Take him to the Infanta's bed-chamber. I'll be waiting there for you.'

Bartolomé allowed the collar to be put around his neck and let himself be led on the lead. He scuttled along behind Marie Barbola through the passageways. Two pages were waiting at the bedroom door.

'So this is supposed to be a dog, Moonface?' they jeered.

Bartolomé bared his teeth and growled menacingly. If these lads annoyed him again, he'd bite. He was a proper dog now. The pages shrank back. Marie Barbola laughed softly.

'Just you watch it,' she warned them. 'He bites people he doesn't like.'

Before the pages could answer, Maria Augustina opened the door.

'You can come in,' she said, and her pretty little face was bright with excitement. It had been ages since she'd had such a great idea.

Marie Barbola marched into the bed-chamber, pulling Bartolomé behind her.

The princess shrieked when she saw the extraordinary little dog. With one leap, she was out of bed and was running barefoot towards Bartolomé. The ladies and gentlemen present clapped delightedly.

Bartolomé suddenly took fright. So many people were staring at him. He tried to hide behind Marie Barbola. He wished he could be invisible.

'Behave yourself,' hissed the dwarf woman at him in disgust, pulling hard on the lead.

The leather collar was choking Bartolomé. But he had a part to play. He couldn't get away. As he'd practised, he sat up on his hind legs and gave a soft bark.

Margarita knelt down in front of him and gave him a rapturous hug.

Bartolomé's heart was beating so hard, he thought it might burst.

'My dear, sweet, funny little dog,' cried Margarita and stroked Bartolomé's head.

When she looked at him with her big blue eyes, Bartolomé forgot that he wasn't really a dog and didn't even want to be one. When the princess gently stroked his nose and cheeks and tickled him under the chin, he stuck out his tongue and gave her rosy little hand a careful lick.

He could hear Marie Barbola giving a horrified gasp behind him. She hadn't practised this trick with him. What Bartolomé was doing was cheeky. The Infanta was sure to push him away in disgust, and the dwarf woman would bear the brunt of her anger.

'Oh!' murmured Margarita in surprise. None of her other animals had ever been so gentle and trusting. She hugged the little dog harder, and Bartolomé could feel her heart beating just as fast as his own.

'Tonight,' Margarita decided, 'he'll sleep beside my bed. Please make a soft bed out of cushions for him.'

BARTOLOMÉ'S little body sank into the thick, soft pillow that a chambermaid had laid next to the bed. In the room, it was dark except for a little oil lamp in a corner, where a lady sat whose job it was to watch over the Infanta all night long as she lay in bed.

Margarita was so overjoyed by this droll little human dog that she couldn't get to sleep.

She turned onto her side and dropped her arms down to Bartolomé and felt the velvet costume. She stroked it and whispered endearments.

Who knows? thought Bartolomé, who was already half asleep. *Maybe this little princess and I can really be friends.*

This thought continued into his dream. He was running through the palace corridors, holding the princess's hand. Sometimes they stood still. They laughed and then the Infanta whispered her little secrets to him. In the dream, Bartolomé had no hump, no club feet and no weak, crooked legs. He was still small, a dwarf, but properly formed and dressed in a page's costume. But in the dream, the pages had to crawl on all fours and perform tricks.

Friendship

WHEN Bartolomé woke, his limbs were aching. The soft pillows had given his deformed body no support during the night. With difficulty, he crawled out of bed. He badly needed to go to the toilet. He looked around him.

The Infanta was still asleep. Her pretty face lay peacefully on a snow-white pillow, framed in blond curls. Her cheeks were pink and she was smiling slightly in her sleep.

The lady-in-waiting who had sat up all night in a corner, in the light of an oil-lamp, had nodded off over her embroidery.

What should he do? Should he just open his buttons, wriggle out of his costume, and relieve himself quietly in a corner? He didn't dare.

He squeezed his legs together and tried to wait. The pressure was becoming unbearable. He crept painfully over to the lady-in-waiting and tugged gently at her dress. She leapt out of her sleep with a start.

'Is something wrong with the Infanta? Does she need me?' she said in panic.

'I'm bursting,' murmured Bartolomé, embarrassed.

'What?' The lady-in-waiting looked at him in consternation. What made this ugly thing think he could bother her with something like this?

'I'm going to go in my costume any minute,' Bartolomé said, suppressing a sob.

'Control yourself.' The lady-in-waiting stood up in disgust. 'Come with me!'

She went to the door and opened it. A guard came running immediately.

'Take him to the privy,' she ordered.

Turning to Bartolomé she said forcefully, 'This is not to happen again. While you are with the Infanta, you are not to express any needs. That won't do.'

Bartolomé nodded unhappily as he crept past her. He needed to go so badly, he could hardly move forward. The soldier could see this and he felt sorry for him. As soon as the door closed behind then, he picked Bartolomé up and ran with him to an outhouse in the yard.

'You know your way back,' said the soldier and left him alone.

In the bare little room, Bartolomé fumbled with his buttons and wriggled out of his dog-pelt as fast as he could. When he was finished and was putting on the costume again, he heard the door being burst open behind him.

'What are you doing here and who are you?' asked an unfamiliar, bossy voice.

Bartolomé turned around. In front of him stood a child, a boy, hardly seven years old. He was wearing an elegant dark red velvet suit. Under it he wore black stockings and a black shirt with white lace at the collar and on the sleeves. The boy had long brown hair and a slim body. Bartolomé tried to cover himself with his pelt.

'What are you putting on?' asked the child. It had to be a page. His clothing was too fine and his voice too confident for a servant.

'A costume,' answered Bartolomé, embarrassed. He didn't want to be mocked again.

'Why?'

'Because I'm playing a human dog for the Infanta,' Bartolomé admitted.

'You were with the Infanta?' The page's face darkened.

Bartolomé nodded. 'I slept in her room.'

'In her room! You're lying! Nobody sleeps with the Infanta, and certainly not someone as ugly as you.'

Bartolomé couldn't stand for this. He thought of the endearments the little princess had used, her smile, the joy he had brought her.

'She likes me. She wants to be my friend,' said Bartolomé, sure of himself.

'Your friend?'

'Absolutely.'

Bartolomé had managed to wriggle back into the costume and to put up his hood. He felt in charge of the situation.

The page spat in his face. 'I, Nicolasito Pertusato, am the Infanta's only friend. She likes me. I'm her favourite dwarf.'

Favourite dwarf? Bartolomé stared at the boy. Really! He suddenly realised that Nicolasito's facial features were not round and soft, but were set and hardened. He noticed a dark film of hair on his upper lip. Nicolasito was not a child but a dwarf like himself, and he must be a few years older than Joaquín.

Bartolomé wiped the spittle off his face with his sleeve. Nicolasito came a step nearer. Bartolomé shrank back. He could sense the anger of this dwarf and he was afraid.

'She loves only me! I'm allowed to pick flowers for her and

to put sweets into her mouth!' cried Nicolasito. 'Tell me, what did she allow you to do?'

'She embraced me and stroked me and whispered endearments to me as I lay by her bed on a pillow.'

'You're lying again! The Infanta does not embrace such creatures. That would disgust her.'

Bartolomé shook his head and said nothing. This could not be true.

'Do you not believe me? Take Marie Barbola. When the Infanta wants to be spooked, she asks for Moonface. That's her job, to scare her.'

'That's not true,' Bartolomé argued. 'She meant it. I have to get back to her. She is waiting for me.'

'We'll go together.'

Nicolasito pulled him up and dragged him by the floppy ears of his costume through the yard into the palace to the Infanta's bedroom.

'We'll ask her. She can decide for herself who she likes and who not.'

'We can't do that!' cried Bartolomé, horrified. He was remembering the strict instructions of the first lady-in-waiting. Nobody was allowed to speak to the Infanta.

'Ha!' crowed Nicolasito. 'I can do that!'

The sentry was standing in front of the great double door which was upholstered in blue velvet.

'That took you long enough!' he snapped at Bartolomé. 'The Infanta is awake. Her ladies will be here in a moment to dress her.'

'Sentry, let us through!' Nicolasito said to him.

He'll get a clip on the ear for this cheek, thought Bartolomé.

A simple dwarf could not give an order to a sentry. But he was wrong. The sentry nodded briefly, stood aside and opened the door. Nicolasito strode in imperiously. Bartolomé followed him slowly, hesitating.

The heavy curtains had been pulled aside and sunlight flooded through the high windows into the room. The little princess was sitting up in bed, nibbling titbits out of a bowl. A lady-in-waiting was standing beside her and a serving girl was filling a washbasin with hot water. Nicolasito took one leap onto the big bed. The eiderdown billowed up. The Infanta laughed.

'Nicolasito, I've missed you so much.'

She offered him a white sugar biscuit. Nicolasito shook his head silently and pouted.

'Are you cross with me?' asked Margarita.

Nicolasito nodded.

'Have I hurt you in some way?' asked the little princess, concerned.

'The Infanta of Spain has broken my poor heart,' replied Nicolasito accusingly.

'How?' cried the little girl, horrified. 'You were fine yesterday morning, and since then we haven't seen each other.'

'Exactly!'

Nicolasito pointed an accusing finger at Bartolomé, who was now cowering on the cushion beside the bed.

'This creature claims he has gained your favour. I didn't believe him, but he insisted that he had been embraced by my Infanta and stroked by her. She is supposed to have whispered many endearments in his ear yesterday evening.'

Margarita laughed loudly. 'But Nicolasito, that's only my

human doggy. He is so funny and he can do tricks. I saw him yesterday afternoon when I was out. I rescued him from the gutter and he is so grateful to me for that.'

'He is a dwarf, an ugly dwarf,' said Nicolasito peevishly.

'He is not like you. Look at him. He's like a real dog, and I love him like a dog,' Margarita explained to her playmate.

Nicolasito remained silent. This was not enough.

Margarita crept over the bedclothes to him and hugged him.

'I love *you* like a proper person,' she breathed into his ear.

Bartolomé heard it anyway. That was the way it was, then. He was only an animal, not a friend.

'If I ask the Infanta nicely,' said Nicolasito slyly, 'will she give up her human dog for the sake of her dwarf?'

Bartolomé's heart skipped a beat. If the Infanta rejected him, would he be thrown out into the gutter and left to rot? That had been what Marie Barbola had said.

The Infanta looked thoughtfully from Nicolasito, her strange dwarf friend, to Bartolomé, her beloved human dog. Of course the doggy was not so important. She couldn't talk to him and play with him as she could with Nicolasito. On the other hand, he was so trusting.

Bartolomé met the Infanta's gaze. This little girl could make a decision that affected his life. He stood up and begged and barked softly.

'Oh, Nicolasito, look how sweet he is!' cried Margarita, charmed. 'He's not doing you any harm. Could you not like him just a little, for my sake?'

Nicolasito considered. If he insisted on getting his way, the princess would give up the other dwarf. On the other hand, she would tire of him eventually anyway.

'Oh, all right,' he said, giving in. 'But the Infanta must not spoil it. Otherwise it will misbehave. A dog has to be made to be obedient at all times.'

The princess embraced her dwarf. 'Nicolasito, you will be in charge of my dog's education!' she announced.

Heaven and Hell

OVER the next few days Bartolomé got used to the routine of the Infanta's court. It was of no interest to the many ladies-in-waiting, chamberlains and teachers and tutors who surrounded the Infanta that he was being worn down by Nicolasito's educational torments on the one hand and Marie Barbola's efforts on the other to teach him more and more exciting tricks in order to retain the interest of the Infanta.

Every time Infanta Margarita showed too much favour to her doggy, Bartolomé was punished afterwards by Nicolasito. He spent hours locked up and hungry in dark rooms and had to put up with being beaten. Nicolasito had requested, and got, a little whip for just this purpose.

And when Nicolasito got fed up with him, Marie Barbola was standing by. She was Maria Augustina de Sarmiento's loyal assistant. The imaginative lady-in-waiting kept thinking up new dramatic sketches for Bartolomé to perform. He had to climb over obstacles and carry little baskets with sweets or flowers for the Infanta.

One day, when a knife-thrower came to perform at court, it was Bartolomé, rigid with fear, who had to act as his target. With a cloth covering his eyes, the performer threw his long, pointy knives at the wooden board in front of which Bartolomé sat stock-still. The Infanta clapped her hands delightedly as the knives landed in the wood to the right and left of Bartolomé. Afterwards, she rewarded the knife-thrower with a coin and Bartolomé with a sticky sweetmeat. For the rest of the evening, he had to lie at her feet and was constantly praised and petted for his bravery. When the Infanta finally let him go, Nicolasito locked him into a cupboard.

The only nice part of Bartolomé's routine were his visits to the artists' studio. Every time his make-up needed touching up, he was taken to Andrés, the apprentice painter. Andrés seemed to understand how much Bartolomé looked forward to this. He dawdled on purpose and found excuses to keep Bartolomé waiting, so that the dwarf had time to have a good look around and recover from all the little cruelties that had been inflicted on him since his last visit to the studio.

The studio consisted of a suite of rooms in Quarto del Principe, that part of Alcázar in which the king resided with his court. Philip the Fourth was very interested in painting and he quite often looked in on Master Velázquez. The court painter had a whole lot of painters and apprentices working for him. Painting was a skill that had to be acquired according to very exact specifications.

There was a lot to be done before a picture could be painted. Canvas had to be stretched and prepared, paintbrushes had to be made and paint powders ground. All this was work for apprentices like Andrés. After these preparations, the master made a sketchy drawing in Indian ink on the greyish-white canvas. His models needed to sit only briefly at this stage, because Don Velázquez had the gift of being able to keep the details of facial features and clothing as an image in his head.

After that, he left the next stages of the work to his apprentices. They painted light and shadows and all the undertones that would not be visible in the final picture but which nevertheless influenced the coloration of the picture. Juan de Pareja, the master's personal assistant, was allowed to paint the draperies and clothes. But since he did not have the master's gift for memorising clothes, wooden models were dressed in the royal family's gorgeous outfits and surrounded by draperies. Juan de Pareja then painted them. Andrés was at his side and it was his job to prepare the required paints.

'He can distinguish shades that I can't see,' Andrés complained to Bartolomé. Juan de Pareja, irritated, had given the apprentice back a palette with shades of red tones, because the differences between the shades of paint were, in his opinion, not graduated finely enough.

Bartolomé was happy. For the next hour, Andrés would have no time to make him up. Swearing softly, Andrés cleaned the palette of smeared paint and started again from scratch.

Bartolomé watched with interest as Andrés ground the various red pigments, one at a time, on the grinding glass and used a spoon to mix them to a thick paste with linseed oil, spirit gum and Venetian turpentine. Red ochre, Spanish red, Persian red, terra cotta, raddle, cinnabar, carmine – he had a whole range of red pigments at his disposal. As he worked, Andrés kept looking at the dark red draperies embroidered in light red, over which played sunlight and shade from the large windows and which glowed in constantly changing shades of red. According to the amount of pigment he used, the shade of red was deeper or paler. He added a little white lead to each paint.

'That makes them glow more,' he explained.

Bartolomé tried to learn all the shades and their names and to keep the amounts and the method used to mix them in his head. When Andrés saw the light in Bartolomé's eyes, he got another sheet of grinding glass and a pestle, and, unnoticed by Master Velázquez, Juan de Pareja and the others, Bartolomé ground paint under Andrés' guidance. Together, they created a new palette. Juan de Pareja was satisfied.

'Is he a good painter?' Bartolomé dared to ask Andrés, as they washed the tools they had been using.

'He is the third best in the studio. Only Don Velázquez and his son-in-law Juan Bautista Martínez del Mazo are more talented.'

'Juan Bautista Martínez del Mazo?'

'You don't know him. He is working in Torre de la Parada, where he is putting a new varnish on a couple of Don Velázquez's pictures. That's why Juan de Pareja is allowed to do so much of the work on this picture in the studio. Otherwise, Don Mazo would be doing it.'

'So are they not allowed to paint their own pictures?' asked Bartolomé, watching Juan de Pareja, who was patiently painting the red embroidery with a fine paintbrush.

'Sometimes, when things are quiet. But it is a much greater honour for them to work under the court painter. Especially for Juan de Pareja.'

'Why?'

'Have you not noticed his dark skin? He is a moor. In fact, he used to be a slave. Don Velázquez only gave him his letter of freedom a few years back.'

'A slave can become a painter?' Bartolomé could hardly believe it.

'Why not? He has mastered the craft to the highest level and he is talented. That's what counts. Don Velázquez even took him as his personal assistant on a study trip to Italy.'

'Andrés,' asked Bartolomé shyly, 'could a dwarf like me also become a painter? I probably shouldn't say so, but I have learned to read and write.'

Andrés laughed merrily. What gave the little lad this strange idea? But then he looked at Bartolomé. His laughter had hurt the dwarf like Nicolasito's whip. He bent down and put a comforting arm around Bartolomé.

'It's not impossible. But very difficult. It helps that you have already learnt to read and write, but an apprentice has very hard work to do. You have to make paper, you have to cover enormous wooden boards with gesso, prime canvases and, of course, keep the studio tidy, and sweep and clean.'

'I can't do that,' Bartolomé conceded sadly.

'Would you like to be a painter?' asked Andrés cautiously. He didn't want to upset Bartolomé even more.

'Before, in the village, I used to draw in the dust with my finger. In Madrid, I once drew on a sheet of paper with pen and ink. And now that I see all these paints, I wish I could paint with them.'

Andrés smiled. Bartolomé was still a child, a sad child with a child's dream. He wanted to make something colourful.

'You don't have to become a painter to do that, Bartolomé,' Andrés assured him. 'Recently, a primed board got a crack in it. It wouldn't put anyone out if I take a piece of it. The next time you come, I'll give you an old palette with nice bright colours. You can sit in a corner and you can paint a picture on the board.'

'Really?'

'It's a promise! And now I'll make you up quickly before one of those ladies-in-waiting comes looking for you, or maybe even the Infanta herself.'

Bartolomé kept quite still while Andrés smeared a thick layer of brown paint on his face. From where he was sitting, he could see Don Velázquez putting the finishing touches to a picture. The figure on the canvas, the gaunt face of which Bartolomé recognised as that of the king, had been painted in a grey outline. Now the master used light brushstrokes to layer the colour on. Bartolomé strained his eyes, but from this distance he couldn't tell what shades the master used for the face of the king.

'What kind of brown has Don Velázquez got on his palette?' he asked.

Andrés looked over briefly.

'He hasn't got any brown. For skin, we use red and white or yellow and white in alternating thin layers, and where a shadow falls, you have to use a little Veronese green. But it's difficult. You mustn't mix the colours, but instead you must put them on in layers and every layer must show through the one on top of it. It's called catching the light.'

White, yellow, red, even green, Bartolomé thought, *that's what a painter needs to make the colour of skin. And not mixed, but in layers over each other.* How wonderful it would be if he could learn that – like Andrés!

Instead, new humiliations awaited him in the chambers of the Infanta. Marie Barbola came running up to him in the corridor.

'This afternoon, the princess is going to a bullfight in the Park of Buen Retiro,' she cried excitedly. 'You are to accompany her. Nicolasito has something special planned for you. He wouldn't tell me what it was.' The dwarf woman made an angry face.

Bartolomé was scared. If Nicolasito was keeping an idea secret from the others, it could only be something bad.

'Do I have to go?' he asked, though he had long since come to the realisation that he never had a choice.

'I wish I could go,' Marie Barbola admonished him. 'You're going to be allowed to travel in the royal coach and you'll be able to see everything from the royal box. The king himself is even going to be present.'

Bartolomé was carried by a guard to the coach, which was already standing in the inner courtyard. His father was sitting up on the coachman's seat. Not even the smallest sign of recognition showed itself in Juan Carrasco's stony demeanour as his son was lifted up into the coach. A little later, the Infanta climbed in, followed by Doña de Ulloa and Nicolasito. The coach set off with a lurch.

Nicolasito smiled evilly at Bartolomé when the Infanta and Doña de Ulloa were not looking. In spite of the heat, Bartolomé shivered.

'What have you planned for me today?' Margarita asked her dwarf friend curiously.

'If I tell you, then it won't be a surprise for the Infanta,' he said.

'Just a little clue!' wheedled the princess.

'The human doggy,' said Nicolasito. 'It's going to have a performance!'

'Really?' The little girl looked at him in surprise.

'Yes. Perhaps he will soon be known as the bravest dog in Spain!' laughed Nicolasito.

Bartolomé pressed himself back into the cushions. Nicolasito bent over him and breathed, 'Or the opposite!'

Bartolomé wished he could disappear.

The Bullfight

THE Infanta Margarita sat beside her father in the gallery. She was so excited that she kept pulling at the pink tulle roses that decorated her dress. The courtiers had all taken their places. In front of Margarita lay a moat with a high wooden fence beyond it, so high that she couldn't see over it. There was a steep wooden slide into the water, and the bellowing and stamping of bulls could be heard from the other side of the fence.

King Philip loved this form of bullfighting. A bull would be driven up a ramp to the top of the slide, which had been rubbed with fat. The terrified animal would try in vain to find its footing on the top of the slide, and would slither helter-skelter down the slide and into the water, where the bullfighters would be waiting in little boats, ready to kill the bull with their knives and lances. Sometimes an animal would manage to make it to the bank, but the wooden fence prevented it from getting away, and bullfighters on horseback would force it back into the water, where it would die, either from its wounds or by drowning.

The little Infanta had often watched bullfights with her father. He had told her about the nasty bulls and the brave toreadors, and Margarita was too small to understand the torment of the bulls. The blood just looked a nice shade of red to her, and the fearful bellowing of the animals sounded like fierce war cries.

'When is it going to start?' she asked impatiently.

Philip the Fourth was proud of his pretty daughter. 'I've heard that your dwarf has a surprise for you before the fight starts,' he said.

Margarita nodded, so that her blond hair fluttered about her head. 'He's got my little dog with him and it's going to be really exciting, he promised.'

The king gave a satisfied nod. Even though Nicolasito was only a dwarf, he came up with the most amazing ideas.

Hidden by the wooden fence, Nicolasito was standing by the ramp that led up to the slide. Beside him sat Bartolomé, his crooked back leaning against a crate from which he could hear the snorting and snarling of a bull. Like a little general, Nicolasito outlined his plan to the lads who were standing around. 'You are to drive it up the ramp, like a bull, till it's up at the top.'

Horrified, Bartolomé stared at Nicolasito. This 'it' he spoke of was him.

'When I give you the nod, you give it a good hard push, and it will go sliding down into the water.'

'Nicolasito, you mustn't do that. I can't swim!' cried Bartolomé.

Nicolasito gave an unconcerned laugh. 'All dogs can swim. It comes naturally to them.'

'I'm not a dog,' protested Bartolomé. 'I'll drown.'

'That's your hard luck,' said Nicolasito.

He wasn't going to let Bartolomé drown. On the contrary. His plan was that he himself would be waiting in a boat and would reach Bartolomé a helping hand. The Infanta would enjoy Bartolomé's adventure, and would admire Nicolasito as a brave hero. But Nicolasito took care not to let Bartolomé know this. The human dog's fear and confusion had to be genuine.

He left Bartolomé in the charge of the lads, and went off to get into a boat.

'Don't pay any heed to him!' pleaded Bartolomé.

'And bring down the anger of the Infanta on us all, for the sake of a weird dog?' said one, shaking his head.

They all laughed and drove him up the ramp with their lances. Up on the wooden platform, Bartolomé tried frantically to hang on. In front of him lay the short steep slide, gleaming with fat. Below, the water was making little green waves. Bartolomé couldn't see the boat, only the water. He couldn't see or hear the seething crowd of spectators. He didn't hear Margarita screaming shrilly, 'That's my little dog! Look, it's climbed up! I hope it's not going to fall in!'

But that was exactly what happened. On a signal from Nicolasito, one of the lads gave Bartolomé a hard push with a wooden pole. Bartolomé went tumbling helplessly down the slide. He could find nothing to cling to. It was over before he could cry out. The dark water closed over his head. He trod water. An air pocket in his costume buoyed him up. Panting for air, he came back up to the surface.

Rowed by an oarsman, the boat carrying Nicolasito came towards him. Nicolasito stretched out his hand. Bartolomé took hold of it. Nicolasito was almost pulled into the water himself. The crippled dwarf in his wet costume was much heavier than he had expected. With the help of the oarsman, he finally managed to pull Bartolomé on board, where he lay, gasping for air and spitting out water, between the benches.

Beaming, Nicolasito raised his arms to take the applause. He was unaware that his little performance fooled nobody except the Infanta. In her eyes, he had performed a heroic deed.

As Nicolasito brought her the streaming wet and shivering Bartolomé, she hugged him and kissed him on both cheeks. But she had no words of endearment for Bartolomé.

'How could you have been so stupid as to run away and climb up there?' she upbraided him. 'I was so scared. If Nicolasito hadn't been so brave, you'd have drowned.'

Bartolomé looked dumbly at Nicolasito, at Doña de Ulloa, even at the king. But nobody on the gallery thought it necessary to explain to the little Infanta what had really happened. Wet through, Bartolomé had to lie at her feet and wait till the whole bullfight was over. When the little company was finally accompanied to the coach, Bartolomé was not allowed to sit inside.

'It's dirty, wet and ugly,' said the Infanta, wrinkling her nose. 'All its colours have run. Let it sit outside with the coachman.'

And so Bartolomé was lifted up to his father, who put a clumsy arm around him so that he wouldn't be jostled from his seat by the swaying of the coach over the uneven ground. He had tried to forget Bartolomé, and he would have succeeded only that he was constantly aware of Isabel's unspoken longing for this child. But this afternoon, when he saw the water closing over the little lad's head, he would have climbed the wooden fence himself to save him, without so much as a thought for his job, if Nicolasito hadn't got there first. Juan could feel Bartolomé shivering, and he held him close.

'Papa,' whimpered Bartolomé.

'Oh, son, if only you had stayed at home in the village, you'd have spared yourself and all of us a lot of grief. Here you are tormented. And your mother sits at home and cries because she misses you. If I told her how they treated you, she would go mad.'

The village, thought Bartolomé. It was so far away, it might as well be on the far side of the moon. It was like a half-forgotten dream. Would he really like to go back there? Even at that moment, when he felt so miserable, he couldn't imagine himself sitting day in, day out, in front of the church, doing nothing.

'There is nobody I can have a word with to make all this stop,' said Juan softly. 'Believe me, Bartolomé, I would do it if I could.'

'Thank you, Papa,' said Bartolomé. He closed his eyes to conjure up the image of his family: the sweet, soft face of his mother; Joaquín's lively eyes; Ana's slim form; Beatríz's pouting mouth and Manuel's rosy baby face. It was lovely, and at the same time sad, to know that his father wanted to take him home but could not do so.

Pictures

NOBODY thought to give Bartolomé dry clothes. Naked and shivering, he had to wait in Marie Barbola's room until most of the wet had been wrung from his costume. Then he put on the damp, cold costume again. Hungry, he cowered on the sofa. He wished he had a nice cosy quilt.

Later, a satisfied Marie Barbola came back from supper. Nicolasito's amusing account of the story had been greeted with great applause.

'Nicolasito is now the absolute favourite of the Infanta,' she announced. 'He wants you to be banished from court as a punishment for causing the princess anxiety. We'll have to think of something that will make the Infanta forgive you.'

'Marie Barbola, I'm hungry and I'm cold,' Bartolomé ventured to interrupt. The dwarf woman wasn't listening.

'You will have to express your gratitude to Nicolasito for rescuing you, in front of the Infanta. That will charm her and soften her up.'

Be grateful to Nicolasito! Never. Bartolomé couldn't do it.

'Well!' Marie Barbola shrugged her shoulders. 'As far as the Infanta is concerned, you were disobedient. And Nicolasito saved your life. That's all that counts.'

Why does nobody take my side? Bartolomé thought.

The following day, he was sent to the studio.

'You're back very quickly,' said Andrés, pleased. He looked into Bartolomé's face, which was smeared with messed-up make-up.

'Have you been swimming, or what?' he joked.

The story about the bullfight evidently hadn't reached the studio. The painters kept themselves aloof from court gossip. Bartolomé lowered his gaze. What was the point of telling Andrés the truth? He couldn't help him.

Andrés hunkered down in front of him and took Bartolomé's face in his hands. 'Did they hurt you?' he asked, concerned.

'Nicolasito tried to drown me. He had me thrown into the water. He said that dogs can swim.' Bartolomé looked beseechingly at Andrés. 'But I'm not a dog.'

'No, you're not,' Andrés said soothingly.

He got a bowl of warm water and a clean cloth. He washed Bartolomé's face carefully. The make-up had left flaky red blotches on his skin.

If he has to go around much longer with a painted face, those are going to get inflamed, thought Andrés. He took a little nut oil and rubbed it carefully over the raw spots.

'Do you know what?' he suggested, 'I won't paint your face until the afternoon. You can stay here until then and ...' Andrés remembered his promise. He knew how to cheer the sad little creature up. 'You can make your own picture.'

He gave Bartolomé a small primed wooden board, a palette on which there was plenty of leftover paint, and an old paintbrush. Bartolomé hardly dared to start. For a while, his gaze hovered from palette to board, and around the studio. What should he do? He only had this one board, this one palette, and very likely only this one chance to make his own picture.

155

'You'd better start,' Andrés said. 'The paints will dry out if you hesitate too long.'

Bartolomé dipped his paintbrush into the dark green. He had no ink to make a preliminary sketch. He had to use the paints immediately. He thought of the pine trees when they had eventually reached the mill on the first day of their journey from the village. He started to paint. He tried to find the right colours.

Never mix, but layer the paints on the picture. Andrés' words came back to him. Bartolomé tried it and managed it. Slowly, a picture emerged. The mighty trees ranged, brownish black, against the evening sky. But if you looked carefully, you could see the green of the pines shimmering through. In the same way, the sky was not just black, but underneath, Bartolomé had painted the red of the setting sun, the white of individual clouds and a deep blue.

Bartolomé wondered whether he should envelop the white mill in a twilight grey. He decided against it. Gleaming white, it shone out of the picture as if it had caught the last light of day and was not ready to release it. With a thin brush, he added details. The laden cart, the donkey, his parents and siblings. Even the chest, waiting, half-open, for him.

He did not notice how often Andrés stood behind him and for how long he stood there and looked over his shoulder. Andrés had not thought that the crippled dwarf could really make a picture. Of course, there were lots of things wrong with it. The mill's water wheel was too big and so crooked that it would fly off and bang against the wall of the house if it were set in motion. The donkey's legs grew out of his body in the wrong places, and the cart stood with only one wheel touching the ground. But the light and the colours made an impression on him. He beckoned the other apprentices to come and look, and, as Bartolomé put the finishing touches to his work and looked up, he was surrounded by five young lads.

They had kept silent as long as he was painting. But now they started to discuss the picture. They crouched down to Bartolomé, clapped him on the back and praised him.

'Andrés says you've never painted a picture before?' one of them asked.

Bartolomé nodded, embarrassed.

'Then you have talent, a lot of talent,' he said.

The others supported him.

'Don't waste it,' counselled Léon, the eldest among them, who was himself working on his master project, which he was planning to submit to Don Velázquez and the representatives of St Luke's Guild, the guild of painters, which upheld the highest standards.

Bartolomé looked from one to the other. They stood around him in their paint-spattered smocks as if he were their equal. Did none of them notice that he was a dwarf, a cripple in a crumpled doggy costume? Even Andrés seemed to have forgotten that. He was discussing with Léon the best varnish for Bartolomé's picture. All the same, Andrés himself had admitted that Bartolomé could never become a painter.

'The varnish must protect the picture, and it needs a frame so that it can be hung,' Andrés was saying, thinking aloud.

Bartolomé interrupted him. 'Andrés, stop. I can't own a picture.'

'Of course you can. If I give it to you, nobody can take it away from you. You can hang it in your room.'

'Andrés, I haven't got a room. I sleep mostly in Marie Barbola's room on the floor beside the sofa. Sometimes on a cushion in the Infanta's room. And when Nicolasito is punishing me, I have to spend the night in some dark box-room or cupboard.'

Shocked, Andrés said nothing. The other apprentices had suddenly found other things to do.

'You must think me stupid and heartless,' Andrés finally said, embarrassed.

Before Bartolomé could answer him, Juan de Pareja came bursting into the studio.

'Quick, quick!' he commanded. 'Master Velázquez has an idea for a new picture of the Infanta. The king has given his warm approval. There's going to be a sitting immediately. The king himself will be present.'

His eyes fell on Bartolomé.

'What's he doing here? Andrés, make him up quickly and get rid of him.'

In all haste, the apprentices prepared the studio. Half-finished pictures were shoved into the next room. Primed boards and stretched canvases of various sizes were stood up against the wall or propped against pieces of furniture. Léon laid out ink and fine paintbrushes on a high table so that Don Velázquez could make his initial sketch. In the middle of all the fuss, Andrés quickly made up Bartolomé's face with leftover brown paint.

'You'll have to disappear from here now,' he warned Bartolomé when he was finished.

But it was too late. The door was thrown open and a chamberlain announced the king.

'Find yourself a corner to hide in. Make yourself invisible!' whispered Andrés to Bartolomé.

The dwarf crept obediently under a table, against which a large canvas in a rough frame had been propped. Hidden behind it, nobody could see him.

A Masterpiece

THE king's deep voice echoed through the room.

'An extraordinary idea, Velázquez. The little Infanta surrounded by her retinue, visits the studio in which her royal parents are just being painted.'

'Your Majesty, no other European ruler will possess such a picture,' answered Don Velázquez in a quiet voice.

The king wandered through the studio, looking at the completed and half-finished paintings. Don Velázquez followed him. Juan de Pareja and the apprentices stood humbly against the walls. It was a great honour that Philip the Fourth was personally discussing the painting of a new picture with Don Velázquez.

'Is Margarita not coming?' asked the king impatiently after a while.

'Your Majesty, the Infanta is on her way. She'll be here at any moment,' a secretary declared.

And indeed, the doors were thrown open for a second time and the chamberlain announced the Infanta. Margarita ran wildly towards her father. But she stopped short in front of him and curtsied. She was old enough to know that the Spanish Infanta does not throw herself into her father's arms.

But the king had little patience with stiff court procedure. He pulled Margarita into his arms.

'Master Velázquez is going to paint a special picture of you.

Will you be a good girl and keep still?' he asked tenderly.

Margarita nodded.

'I'll send Moonface away, so she won't make me laugh.' She pointed at Marie Barbola, who had accompanied her.

The king shook his head. 'No. For this picture, we need your retinue too. Everyone has to think you've just dropped by the studio by chance with your courtiers.'

Margarita looked around. Maria Augustina de Sarmiento and Isabel de Velasco, her two ladies-in-waiting, Doña Marcela de Ulloa, her first lady-in-waiting, a soldier of her guard of honour, Marie Barbola and, of course, Nicolasito had accompanied her.

'Are they all to be in the picture?' she asked, disbelievingly.

The king gave a happy laugh. 'Exactly, and Don Velázquez himself and José Nieto, your chamberlain, too. Even your mother and I will be visible.'

Margarita pulled a face. 'Then it's not a picture of me.'

'It is, darling. Because you are the focus. We're all just there to support you.'

The little girl pouted. 'I don't want to be painted,' said Margarita to Don Velázquez and she stamped her foot.

Before he could think up an answer, however, Maria Augustina intervened. 'If Master Velázquez paints the Infanta next to Moonface, she will be even more beautiful.' She looked pointedly at Don Velázquez.

He coughed. 'In a way, you are right. In the same way that dark colours make light colours near them seem even brighter ...' He hesitated. 'So the beauty of the Infanta will be even more radiant by comparison with the other people in the picture.'

'You see,' laughed the king, 'because your Papa is so ugly, he has to be in the picture too, so that you are even prettier.'

161

'I don't think you're ugly,' said Margarita seriously.

The king kissed her long blond curls tenderly. 'It is very sweet of you to say so.'

Margarita turned to Don Velázquez. 'Marie Barbola is to stand right next to me,' she ordered. 'She is the ugliest.'

It was the king himself who chose the canvas for the painting. He went around the studio, looking. Finally his gaze fell on the canvas that was propped against Bartolomé's table. Andrés and Léon hurried over to lift up the canvas for the king. Light fell under the table.

'There's my human doggy!' cried Margarita in joyful surprise.

Nicolasito's face darkened with anger. He had hoped that the Infanta would forget about Bartolomé if he disappeared from view for a while. 'We still have to punish him, Infanta,' he reminded her, for all to hear.

'Oh, no,' pleaded Margarita. 'Look how he's crept so guiltily under the table. Come to me. All is forgiven.'

She crouched down and stretched out her arms to the dwarf. Ashamed, Bartolomé crept out from under the table. It was terrible that Andrés and Léon, who had just been admiring his picture, could see now how he had to act as the Infanta's human dog. Margarita gave Bartolomé a big hug. He barked, as he had been told to. His bark was soft and hoarse.

'You've caught a cold,' cried the Infanta.

Bartolomé shook his head. The Infanta dragged him to Don Velázquez.

'My doggy must be in the picture,' she decreed. 'He is the sweetest thing I have.'

From the corner of his eye, Bartolomé caught sight of Nicolasito's face. It was contorted with anger.

Skilfully and courteously Don Velázquez moved the little group around until the king, happy with the arrangement, left the studio. The Infanta was the focal point. To her right and left stood the two ladies-in-waiting and behind her, the first lady-in-waiting and the guardsman. Marie Barbola and Nicolasito were placed to the side. Bartolomé had to lie on the floor in front of Nicolasito. The Infanta gave a loud snort when Nicolasito playfully rested his leg on Bartolomé's crooked back. Don Velázquez frowned but said nothing, and Nicolasito remained, all bluster, in this pose.

'If the Infanta would just keep still for a moment,' Don Velázquez requested politely, 'then I can draw a sketch.'

The first sitting did not take long. After a few minutes, Don Velázquez had drawn the outline and the most important details in Indian ink on the canvas. He thanked the little Infanta, and praised her pretty behaviour. Then she left the studio with her retinue.

Bartolomé had to go too. Marie Barbola, who had watched with pleasure how the Infanta had fussed over Bartolomé, pulled him along behind her.

'Now we're back in her good books,' she whispered excitedly. 'You're even going to be in the picture. Imagine that! There will be a painting of us.'

Nicolasito was walking behind them, listening to what Marie Barbola was saying. 'You two are only included,' he said maliciously, 'because you are so unbelievably ugly.'

DON VELÁZQUEZ guarded his work jealously. It was going to be a masterpiece – perhaps his last, for he had begun to notice the first indications of old age: a more hesitant step, a stiffening in the joints and a decline in the sharpness of his eyesight. Unlike the other paintings, for which the apprentices and assistants did the necessary preparatory work and were allowed to paint in the less important parts, this painting would belong to him alone.

After the first sitting, the Infanta and her noble ladies-in-waiting made no further appearances in the studio. The three dwarves, however, had to be present. They posed for long hours while wooden forms which had been draped with gorgeous garments stood in for the Infanta and her companions.

Marie Barbola put up with all the standing around with an expressionless face. Behind this mask, however, she hid her satisfaction. For the painting, she'd got a new gown of black velvet with silver embroidery and white lace. She was also allowed to wear a precious amber necklace around her neck.

Nicolasito, dressed as a page, was extraordinarily pleased with the pose he had struck for himself. But the longer he had to stand, the more heavily his shoe pressed down on Bartolomé's back. Don Velázquez noticed this sly cruelty and put an end to it. Nicolasito was given a low wooden stool on which he could rest, as Don Velázquez remarked mildly, his foot as heavily as he wished. Nicolasito stared angrily at the court painter, but he didn't dare to say anything.

Don Velázquez turned to Bartolomé. 'You can go. I'll paint you separately. When I need you, I'll send for you.'

Bartolomé gathered up all his courage. 'May I stay and watch?' he asked quietly.

'You'll be bored. It's not interesting for a child.'

'But I really would like to stay,' Bartolomé whispered miserably.

Andrés overheard. He stepped forward and said, 'Master Velázquez, with your permission, he can help me to prepare the paints. He won't be in the way.'

Don Velázquez nodded. As long as the dwarf child didn't get under his feet, and Andrés did not neglect his duties, it was fine with him.

He turned towards the canvas. He couldn't really have been listening. Otherwise, he'd have found it very strange that a dwarf knew how to make paints.

Sittings

DON VELÁZQUEZ needed four sittings to get Marie Barbola and Nicolasito down on the canvas. The sittings took many hours. Hours that Bartolomé was allowed to spend in the studio to his heart's content, as long as he did not get in Master Velázquez's way. Andrés, Léon and the other apprentices accepted him as part of their circle.

There was no fear that he would be summoned to the Infanta's side because, immediately after the first sitting, she had gone with her parents to their country castle, Torre de la Parada, which was situated in the holm oak forest. The hunting season had started and this created an excuse for excursions, drives and rowdy parties.

The apprentices showed Bartolomé how paintbrushes were made out of the fine hairs of pine martens or squirrels, how boards were glued and how canvases were primed with gesso, made from a mixture of chalk, zinc white and limewash. They taught him the difference between oil paints and the tempera with which he was made up.

The best part of all, though, was that he was able to wash his face and take off his dog costume. He got an old painter's smock from Andrés. Hidden from curious eyes behind a canvas, he quickly changed his clothes. The smock covered him completely. Laughing, Andrés cut the sleeves shorter and with a cord, he tied the shirt around Bartolomé's crooked legs to make a pair of baggy trousers of it. Dressed like this, Bartolomé felt like a proper apprentice painter.

He made eager efforts to see, to understand and to learn everything. Even Juan de Pareja, who always kept himself a bit apart from the apprentices, was touched by Bartolomé's thirst for knowledge. When the apprentices could not answer Bartolomé's questions, it was he who crouched down to him and gave him the information he required.

During the third sitting, Bartolomé plucked up the courage to show Juan de Pareja his own painting. Juan de Pareja looked at it for a long time. He could easily have pointed out all the mistakes. But, like the apprentices, he was struck by Bartolomé's choice of colour, by the glowing white mill and by the dark evening landscape through which the shades of day still glimmered.

'Why is it so white?' he asked Bartolomé, putting a brown thumb on the mill.

'I don't know,' answered Bartolomé shyly. 'It just seemed right.'

'That's not enough,' Juan de Pareja chided him. 'A painter must try to puzzle out why.'

Bartolomé thought it over. Why had he painted the mill such a radiant white? In reality, it had been dark grey in the evening light. Maybe that had been a mistake. Should he paint over it in a darker colour?

'Think it over,' said Juan de Pareja, 'and when you know why, come to me. I'd like to know.'

After the fourth sitting, Don Velázquez sent Marie Barbola and Nicolasito away. Then he turned to Bartolomé. 'In the morning, it's your turn.'

Bartolomé nodded.

'Suitably made up and properly dressed,' Don Velázquez aded. He'd only just noticed that the dwarf had taken off his costume.

Bartolomé hung his head. He hated the dog costume, but he had no choice. In the picture, he had to be the Infanta's human dog.

That night, Bartolomé slept secretly in a corner of the studio. Andrés noticed, but he let him be. He was sure that Bartolomé wouldn't do any harm and he wanted to let him have the feeling of being an apprentice painter for a while longer.

The next morning, Bartolomé silently donned his costume. Andrés helped him to button it up.

'It's not so very terrible!' he said, trying to console the dwarf as he began to make up his sad face. 'Just remember, a dog stands for loyalty and courage.'

Bartolomé bit his lip. He was not a dog. He didn't want to be a dog, not even the bravest, most loyal dog in Spain. He wanted to be Bartolomé.

Don Velázquez told him to lie sideways on the floor, to stretch out his arms and legs and to keep his head up.

The master started to paint. Bartolomé paid attention. He'd already seen, when the painter was doing Nicolasito and Marie Barbola, how quickly and confidently Don Velázquez painted the figures with swift brushstrokes.

But this time it didn't work like that. The court painter kept stopping up short. At one point, he went so far as to throw the brush angrily on the table and scrape off the paint he'd applied with a scalpel. He was in a bad mood. It had not been a good idea to include this crippled child in his ridiculous costume in the picture. If only the Infanta had not insisted on it! He'd been able to render the fat dwarf woman and the dainty page with some kind of dignity with his brush – but this!

Bartolomé hung his head. It was tiring to hold it up for so long.

'Stop that,' Don Velázquez snarled at him. Although Bartolomé's muscles ached, he lifted his head again obediently. But not high enough.

'Can you not at least behave like a proper dog? That's not too much to ask, is it?'

Don Velázquez had put down his palette and come near to Bartolomé. He dragged the dwarf's head roughly into the right position.

Bartolomé gave a loud cry of pain. So loud, that the whole studio suddenly fell silent.

Horrified, Don Velázquez let him go. Bartolomé slumped back. His neck and back hurt terribly. He felt as if he could not move his head any more. He felt sick and dizzy. The apprentices and Juan de Pareja came over to him.

'I think I've hurt him. I didn't mean to,' said Don Velázquez contritely.

Juan de Pareja crouched down to Bartolomé and picked him up. He laid him on the table, which Léon and Andrés quickly cleared. In front of everyone, he gently took Bartolomé's costume off and felt his back, neck and shoulders.

Bartolomé started, and suppressed a yell.

'His shoulder is dislocated,' muttered Don Pareja and he started to massage the deformed little back.

'I have to loosen up your muscles and then I can click it back into place for you,' he explained to Bartolomé, who was lying silently on the table with his eyes closed.

Nobody said anything. They had all studied how the body

was structured so that they could paint bodies properly. But even Don Velázquez, the great master, had no idea that there could be such a badly deformed and twisted body under the costume. But he understood what his anger had caused. He saw the way Bartolomé clenched his teeth to prevent himself from crying out again. It was his fault that the dwarf had to suffer this pain.

'I can't paint him as a human dog,' murmured Don Velázquez. He went back to the canvas and carefully removed the layers of paint that showed Bartolomé as a grotesque figure, half-human, half-dog.

Andrés went up to him. 'Don Velázquez?' he said.

The court painter liked Andrés. He reminded him of himself when he had been a pupil.

'What is it, Andrés?' he asked.

'Couldn't you paint Bartolomé as a proper dog, big and strong and beautiful? I've told him that a painter always paints in a dog as a symbol of courage and loyalty. And Bartolomé is very brave.'

'So Bartolomé is his name,' said Don Velázquez thoughtfully.

Andrés waited for an answer. None came. Lost in thought, Don Velázquez reached for a brush and palette.

Dream of the Future

DON VELÁZQUEZ was thinking. If he took up Andrés' suggestion he would run up against the rules of the court. The king had approved the set-up for the picture. There couldn't be any changes to that. On the other hand, could he not paint Bartolomé as the Infanta saw him?

It was impossible. Over the years that he had been the king's painter, he had often painted the court dwarves, but he had always tried to give them their due dignity. People had robbed Bartolomé of his human dignity, however, by dressing him as a dog and making him behave as such.

Don Velázquez reached a decision. *I'll do it*, he thought, and started to paint.

Before Andrés' eyes, a real dog appeared, dark brown, trim, but big and strong.

'It's Jupiter, the king's favourite hunting dog,' said Don Velázquez to Andrés, when he was finished. 'The king will like that. And the Infanta will have to go along with it.' Don Velázquez smiled with satisfaction.

Meanwhile, Juan de Pareja had put Bartolomé's shoulder back in place and Léon had put his painter's smock on him. Don Velázquez went over to them.

'Bartolomé, would you like to see the picture?' he asked.

Bartolomé shook his head. *Never*, he thought.

171

'You should, though,' said Andrés and picked him up from the table with a swift movement. He carried him to the picture.

Bartolomé closed his eyes. 'I don't want to see it,' he said miserably. 'I know how ugly I am.'

'Rubbish. Open your eyes!' replied Andrés. 'Otherwise, I will never let you paint again.'

Reluctantly, Bartolomé opened his eyes. In front of him was the picture.

'It's not me!' he cried. 'It's a real dog. Don Velázquez hasn't painted me.' Relieved, and at the same time upset that he was too ugly to appear in a painting, he looked over at Don Velázquez.

'I did paint you,' the master said.

'I'm not a dog,' said Bartolomé.

'I know, but the Infanta has dressed you as a dog. She only sees your outside appearance. After all, she's only a little girl. We have to forgive her that.' Don Velázquez was choosing his words carefully. 'A painter tries to see what is inside, hidden, and to capture it with his brushstrokes on the canvas.'

'But that's not me,' Bartolomé said stubbornly. Whatever else was going to happen, he decided at this moment never to be a dog again.

Don Velázquez nodded. 'That's right. You are not a dog. For this reason, I could not paint your outer self as the Infanta sees you. So that is why I took your inner self and painted it in the form of Jupiter, the king's favourite hound. Just look at how strong that dog is. That is your strength.'

Bartolomé stared at the dog. Was the dog's outer self really his own inner self? Or was Don Velázquez just trying to console him, a sad, ugly little dwarf?

Bartolomé looked at the picture for a long time. The dog did not look back at him. He lay peacefully under Nicolasito's foot.

All at once, Bartolomé could see what Don Velázquez meant. He saw the dog's strength, the muscles under the smooth, dark brown coat. Nicolasito was not in control of the dog; rather, the dog was good-naturedly tolerating Nicolasito's stuck-up posing.

At any moment, Bartolomé thought, *that dog could have enough of this, leap up and give Nicolasito an unpleasant surprise.* It made him smile.

'You see,' Don Velázquez said contentedly.

Bartolomé nodded. Something suddenly clicked in his head.

'Don Pareja,' he called excitedly to the Moorish painter, who was varnishing a painting nearby. 'I know now why I painted the mill so white in my picture!'

'Your picture?' asked Don Velázquez in surprise.

'Master, I let him paint a picture,' explained Andrés, 'using leftover paints and an old board. The board was no good for anything else.'

Don Velázquez nodded.

'It's a good picture,' added Juan de Pareja. 'Bartolomé has talent.'

He got the picture and showed it to Don Velázquez.

'Why did you paint the mill so white?' he asked.

'Because it was our destination on this long day of travelling. My father planned to arrive in daylight, but we didn't make it. We were too slow. By the time we arrived, it was dark, but even so, the milled seemed white in my memory, rather than grey. As if it hung on to the daylight a bit longer, to show the travellers that they had reached their destination, safe and sound, and could stay there overnight.'

Suddenly shy, Bartolomé stopped. This idea was probably stupid and childish. Andrés and Léon would laugh at it.

'The way a painter thinks,' said Juan de Pareja admiringly.

'Really?' asked Bartolomé, astonished.

Everyone around him nodded in agreement. Even Don Velázquez.

'You have the makings of a painter, Bartolomé,' Juan de Pareja said.

'Dwarves can't become painters,' said Bartolomé softly. 'Even if they want to very badly.'

'Who said that?' asked Don Velázquez.

'I did,' admitted Andrés. 'How could Bartolomé drag buckets of gesso around the place, learn to make paper, carry wooden boards, stretch canvases, frame paintings and, last but not least, clear up the studio?'

'A painter has his apprentices for that kind of donkey work,' Don Velázquez said.

Andrés flushed. 'I don't want to be awkward,' he said, 'but anyone who wants to be a painter has to be an apprentice first.'

'Or perhaps not,' said Don Velázquez quietly.

'And how could he paint large pictures?' asked Andrés.

'He could specialise in miniatures,' Don Velázquez came back at him.

'What painter would take him on under those conditions? And what would the guild have to say?' Léon chipped in, thinking of the examination he was going to have to do shortly.

Don Velázquez said nothing. Every painter had to be approved by the Guild of St Luke. It was unthinkable that they would recognise Bartolomé as a painter without the appropriate training. It was equally unthinkable that Bartolomé could learn the craft in accordance with the guild's rules.

'You see,' said Andrés. 'Not even you, the king's court painter, could take Bartolomé on as an apprentice. Bartolomé simply can't become a painter, even though he is so talented.'

Bartolomé, in whom a vague hope had started to grow during this exchange, now balled his fists.

'I'm so fed up with it all!' he cried. 'Some people hurt me because they hate me, others because they don't care about me one way or another, and you ...'

'And we've hurt you because we gave you a hope that cannot be realised,' Juan de Pareja finished his sentence for him.

Bartolomé nodded. A single tear ran down his cheek.

Andrés and Léon looked away in embarrassment. They liked Bartolomé; they'd like to help him, but there was nothing they could do about the strict rules of the guild.

'Don Velázquez.' Juan de Pareja turned to the court painter. 'Years ago, in Genoa, you bought a slave child in chains because he drew figures in the sand of the marketplace, and set him free. You took me on and taught me the craft of painting, and you took no notice of the Guild of St Luke. I know I can never call myself a painter. I'm not even an apprentice.'

Andrés and Léon looked at Juan de Pareja curiously. They hadn't known that.

'The masters of the guild wouldn't allow me to take the exams, and none of my pictures bears my name,' Juan de Pareja continued. 'As a moor and a former slave I don't have the right to do that. But I have never complained. I've never asked you for anything. It has always been enough for me to serve you. I would take Bartolomé on as a pupil. He can serve me as I serve you. I'll teach him the craft, and no master of the guild can hold it against you.'

Bartolomé beamed at Juan de Pareja. Don Velázquez kept silent for a long time.

'I will allow it, if Bartolomé understands what he is taking on,' said the court painter eventually.

Bartolomé would love to have leapt high in the air. He nodded furiously.

'I want to be a painter,' he cried.

Juan de Pareja picked him up and put him on the table.

'Bartolomé, do you understand what you are letting yourself in for?' he said seriously.

'Yes, and I want to be a painter!'

'You will never be a painter like Léon, Andrés and the others,' said Juan de Pareja curtly. 'You have to understand that people like us – moors, slaves, dwarves – are outside society. We haven't got the same rights. We are not admitted to guilds and associations. We are accorded no privileges. People put up with us only as long as we make ourselves useful and make no demands.'

'That doesn't matter to me,' cried Bartolomé.

'It *should* matter to you! Just imagine what it would be like to make things, day in, day out, that can never belong to you. Someone else will get the credit for everything you do. Everything you paint, and you will paint wonderfully, will be signed by someone else, your pictures will bear a stranger's name.'

'Don Pareja, that is still a hundred times better than the way things are at the moment, when I am not even allowed to be myself. I still want to paint, even if I can never be a painter.'

Bartolomé looked at Don Pareja, who said, 'Right. Well then, from this moment on, you are my pupil.'

The apprentices clapped their hands and carried Bartolomé, beaming with joy, around the studio in triumph.

As the most senior apprentice, Léon baptised Bartolomé with the water in which the brushes were washed, and Andrés gave him a present of a palette.

'When I am my own master,' he promised, 'you can come to me. You can paint the small pictures and I'll paint the big ones. We'll sign them all with a double-barrelled name: Bartolomé Andrés.'

Juan de Pareja and Don Velázquez watched the celebrations.

'It won't be easy for him,' said Don Velázquez quietly.

'It wasn't for me either,' replied Juan de Pareja, 'but he has nothing to lose. Things can only improve for him.'

'The Infanta,' said Don Velázquez thoughtfully. 'She'll probably want him back.'

'Children forget quickly. She hasn't seen him for three weeks. She'll have a new plaything by now.'

'And if not?' asked Don Velázquez.

Juan de Pareja thought it over. 'A wise man once said, if you can't change something yourself, then you can be sure that somebody else will. Fate has to work in Bartolomé's favour at some stage.'

A Real Dog

ON the afternoon that Juan Carrasco had put his arm helplessly around Bartolomé, he went home, knowing that he must rescue his son from the palace and take him back to the village. It had been a terrible mistake to bring him to Madrid.

Juan had to admit that, until now, he had never paid Bartolomé any real attention. The crippled dwarf had remained a stranger to him. Before, on his rare visits to the village, when he saw how much trouble Bartolomé caused Isabel, he had often thought that a child like that should die at birth instead of making everyone else's life difficult. He had been there and had seen the midwife helping a tiny, floppy blue child into the world. The old woman had had to dunk the newborn into a bucket of cold water before the tiny bundle of humanity had started to breathe. Afterwards, she had put the child, naked, into his arms. Juan had looked at it in disgust. The deformed feet, the crooked back which would later become a hump and the oversized head had marked Bartolomé as a cripple from his first breath.

Ana, Joaquín, Beatríz – he was proud of them. But from the very beginning, he had been ashamed of Bartolomé. If Isabel had not loved the baby so much, he would have been all on for leaving him outside a convent as a foundling and abandoning him to his fate. He remembered all that now, as he made his way slowly home through the streets of Madrid.

When he came into the little apartment, his family was waiting for him. Food was steaming on the stove. Manuel ran babbling up to him to be thrown up into the air by his father's strong arms. Juan took no notice of him, however.

Joaquín was home on a visit. Ana and Isabel were sewing at the window and Beatríz was setting the table.

'We have to get Bartolomé out of the palace,' said Juan loudly into the room. 'I cannot stand by while they make him ridiculous and torment him.' He felt relieved now that he had said it.

Isabel leapt up. 'What are they doing to him?' she cried. Until now, Juan had refused to discuss Bartolomé with her.

He sat on the bed.

'The Infanta has had a dog costume made for him, with a tail and floppy ears, and this afternoon ...' Juan faltered. 'This afternoon, they threw him into the water at the bullfight. He would have drowned if someone hadn't rescued him at the last moment.'

Isabel, Ana and Joaquín stared at him uncomprehendingly.

'They treat him like an animal,' Juan went on. 'No, worse than that. A real animal would defend itself. It would bite or scratch. But Bartolomé has to put up with whatever they demand of him.'

'How long have you known this, and why did you not take him away immediately?' Isabel demanded angrily.

Juan covered his face with his hands. He could sense the odium in her accusation.

'How could I do that?' he said softly. 'He is the property of the Infanta. It would be considered theft, and who would look after him and provide for you all if I am in jail?'

'But we have to bring him home!' cried Ana. 'He is not an animal and he does not belong to the Infanta.'

Juan nodded. 'That's what I want too, but I don't know how. The Infanta is besotted with her human dog. She will never give him up.'

'There has to be a way,' murmured Joaquín. 'Suppose we kidnap him and hide him?'

'Impossible. The Infanta's surroundings are under constant surveillance. Nobody gets to her except by order of their Majesties, or under the protection of her first lady-in-waiting.'

'A letter ...' Joaquín did not want to give up. 'Could we not get a letter to Bartolomé, saying that he should flee and that we will be waiting for him outside the palace?'

'Who is to write this letter?'

'Don Cristobal of course! He would definitely help us if he hears how mean they are being to Bartolomé.'

'And who is going to read it to Bartolomé?'

'But he can read!' Ana interjected.

Juan had forgotten. That terrible afternoon came back to him now. If he had not been so furious about Bartolomé's secret lessons, he would certainly never have hit Ana and maybe he would not have taken Bartolomé to the palace either.

'It won't work. I don't know anyone to whom I could entrust a letter. In the palace, there are lots of envious people. Someone would read it, and then I'd end up in jail anyway. That's no good.'

'Has the princess not got a real dog to love?' Beatríz suddenly butted in. She couldn't understand why a princess would want her ugly brother as a dog when there were so many sweet little dogs in Madrid. Only recently, she had been admiring a basket of puppies in the market. Every single one of them was a hundred times cuter than Bartolomé.

Nobody listened to her. But Beatríz was a determined girl. She stood up in front of her father, put her hands by her side and said: 'Papa, I know how we can get Bartolomé back.'

Juan laughed.

'I really do know,' insisted Beatríz.

'How?' asked Ana.

'We'll do a swap,' explained the little girl.

'What are we going to swap?' asked Isabel.

'A dog, of course. We'll swap a real dog for Bartolomé.'

Now they all laughed.

Beatríz stamped her foot. 'What are you laughing about?' she cried unhappily. 'If I were the princess, I would give Bartolomé up immediately for a proper dog.'

Isabel reached out to take Beatríz in her arms, to console her, but Joaquín stood between them. His eyes were shining.

'Why is a proper dog better than Bartolomé?' he asked.

Beatríz looked at her brother in astonishment. It was obvious.

'Bartolomé is so ugly, and he can't walk properly either – and he's not actually a dog,' she explained.

'Of course he's not a dog,' Isabel snapped.

Joaquín signalled to her to keep quiet.

'And a proper dog?' he prompted his sister.

Beatríz could just see the basket of puppies in front of her.

'A proper dog is sweet. I would stroke him and race him. He would sleep beside me. I wish I had a little dog just for me. I'd look after him well.'

She gave her father a longing look. Who knows, maybe he would get her one.

Juan shook his head. 'We have enough problems, Beatríz,' he said. 'We can't afford to feed a dog.'

Joaquín went on thinking. The Infanta and Beatríz were around the same age. She must have the same kind of thoughts and desires as his sister.

'Papa,' said Joaquín. 'If we buy a cute little puppy and give it to the Infanta as a present, then maybe she wouldn't need Bartolomé any more.'

Juan considered it. Could this plan work? He could see that there were a lot of flaws in it.

'Suppose he wets the floor, if he scratches or bites the Infanta or is a bit rough with her?' he asked.

'We would train him well first.'

'And who is going to give the Infanta this dog?'

'Bartolomé,' said Joaquín. 'And he should ask her to take the real dog in his place.'

Juan shook his head. They were back to the original problem.

'How could we get in touch with Bartolomé in secret? How could we give him a dog, if I can't get as much as a letter to him without it being seen by many eyes?'

Joaquín didn't know either. 'There has to be a way. It's just that we can't see it yet,' he said stubbornly.

'We could at least try,' Ana begged her father.

Juan looked at Isabel. 'What do you think? Does it make sense?'

Before Isabel could answer, Beatríz said: 'If the princess is going to get a dog from us, can I have one too? It can share my food.'

Isabel smiled. 'We could give it a try,' she said.

Juan gave in. With two fewer mouths to feed, since Bartolomé and Joaquín had left, he had managed to save a little money, enough to buy a dog. Isabel's horrified reaction had shamed him deeply. If they could free Bartolomé in this way and if he personally could take him back to the village, to Tomáz, where the child would be safe, he would have made up in some way for what he had done.

But what if it didn't work? Juan wavered.

Isabel seemed to be thinking the same thing. 'If it doesn't work, we could always sell the dog again,' she said softly.

'All right, then,' Juan decided. 'We'll give it a try.'

Beatríz sulked when she realised she was not going to get a dog of her own. She didn't want to go with them to the market to choose a puppy for the Infanta. She stood defiantly where she was in the room. Isabel lifted her up.

'You want Bartolomé to come home, don't you?' she asked gently.

Beatríz nodded reluctantly.

'Then you have to help!' said Isabel.

'Why? It was my idea, and now Joaquín is going on as if he was the one who thought of it. And I'm not going to get a dog of my own either.'

Isabel looked at Joaquín.

'Joaquín knows that, don't you, Joaquín?'

'It was Beatríz's idea,' Joaquín conceded readily. 'Are we going to go to the market now? I know a market trader who has puppies.'

'He's doing it again.' Beatríz's lower lip quivered.

'Just a minute,' said Juan. He'd been thinking the plan through quietly. 'Beatríz,' he said, 'not only is it your idea, but the plan can only work if you help.'

'Really?'

183

'You must be the one to choose the little dog.'

'Not Joaquín?'

'Certainly not Joaquín.' Juan turned to face the whole family. 'Do you see? Beatríz has to like the puppy. That's the only way to do it. And we'll have to train the puppy so that it obeys only Beatríz. That way, the Infanta will like it too, and it will obey her. They are both little girls, after all.'

He smiled at Beatríz.

'I'm like the Infanta!' breathed Beatríz.

Isabel hugged her close.

'You are a thousand times better than the Infanta,' she said.

They bought a little puppy with a good pedigree, according to the market trader. What was much more important, though, was that Beatríz chose him as the sweetest of the litter.

At home, they spent days training the puppy together. Juan thanked his lucky stars that the princess's visit to the country was extended by two weeks, and that she had gone there in her parents' coach and did not need him to drive her.

The little dog, which Beatríz christened Justo, learnt quickly. Soon the puppy knew that he was not allowed to leave little puddles indoors, and he came running when Beatríz called him in her clear child's voice. Juan spent a lot of time teaching Justo never to respond to a deep, adult voice. He would put Ana or Beatríz standing at one side of the room, and himself or Isabel on the opposite side. Then they would both call him at the same time. If Justo ran to the girls, he was rewarded with titbits. If he went to the adults, however, he got nothing. It didn't take Justo long to understand what was expected of him.

'I wish we didn't have to give him away,' sighed Beatríz from time to time. Secretly, she wished she really could keep the dog.

Why couldn't her father just ask the Infanta, while they were out driving in the coach, to let Bartolomé go home?

Every time Juan was in the palace, and had time to spare, he tried to get news of Bartolomé. He sought out the company of the guardsmen. He would invite them to a glass of wine and try to get them to talk. But they could tell him nothing about Bartolomé, except that he was the Infanta's human doggy.

Juan did not have much time left. The royal family would soon be coming back to Madrid. Part of the Infanta's little household, under the leadership of the chamberlain, Don Nieto, had already gone to the country house in order to prepare the Infanta for her return journey.

One afternoon, as Juan was cleaning the Infanta's coach in the stables, a page came running in.

'Hurry!' he ordered. 'Get a coach ready for Don Nieto.'

Juan bowed his head. Now was his chance to find out about Bartolomé.

'Sir,' asked Juan, 'I have a clever son. Would it be possible for him to get a place as a page to the Infanta?'

The page gave an arrogant smile.

'My father is Don Rodriguez de Herraro. He owns large tracts of land and is a loyal supporter of the king.'

'So one would have to be of noble blood, like you?' said Juan flatteringly.

The page nodded.

'Only the noblest boys are good enough to serve the Infanta of Spain.'

'Excuse my ignorance, sir, but I have heard that the Infanta has a crippled dwarf as a page. Is he also of noble blood?'

'That's not a page, it's the human dog!' said the boy in disgust.

'Who told you he was a page?'

Juan hid a smile. The page had taken the bait.

'Oh, some drunken guardsman,' lied Juan. 'I wouldn't even know him if I saw him again.'

The page turned away. As far as he was concerned, this conversation was over.

But Juan started up again. 'Would you allow me to ask one more question, sir?'

The page, who hardly counted in the household and was ordered around by everyone, nodded graciously.

'Noble sir, what is a human dog?' asked Juan.

The page laughed.

'That's what the Infanta calls him. Actually, he's just an ordinary dwarf. She rescued him from the gutter and had a dog costume made for him. He has to wear it day and night, and with his brown face, he really does look like a dog. He behaves like a dog too. Sometimes we think he is more dog than human.'

'Brown face? Has he got a disease?' asked Juan.

The stupidity of the lower orders is unbelievable, thought the page. Aloud he said, 'Of course not. He is made up. An apprentice of Don Velázquez, the court painter, is responsible for that.'

A painter's apprentice. Juan made a mental leap in the air. Now he had something to go on.

'How much longer is it going to take to get a coach?' asked the page, suddenly impatient.

'Right away, sir!' Juan hastened to say. 'I'll get a coach and drive it around.'

While Juan was harnessing the horses, he was thinking rapidly. It could not be too hard to find out where in Madrid the painters' apprentices met up. Every guild and association had its own tavern, where its members liked to go to enjoy each other's company. But what should he say to this apprentice? All of a sudden, the plan with the expensive puppy seemed ridiculous. He should not have been persuaded to take part in this scheme.

All the same, he set off that evening to find the tavern.

Andrés

THE tavern in which the painters' guild met was situated in a spacious vaulted cellar. Over the entrance, a wooden paintbrush and a palette were hung on an iron chain. Just inside the door, a staircase led down into the cellar. Smoke, food smells, the murmur of voices and gales of laughter came gusting out onto the street every time the door was opened.

Downstairs, countless oil lamps and candles bathed the tables, benches and chairs in a glimmering light. Business was brisk. Most of the tables were already taken, though it was still early in the evening. The tavern-keeper and two young serving boys were running around with jugs of wine and plates of food. From the kitchen came the loud voice of the tavern-keeper's wife. Every now and again she appeared, tall and stout, behind the counter and gave a good look around the room. There was a picture of her on the wall.

Andrés and Juan de Pareja had found an unoccupied table. They ordered wine with bread and soup.

'The Infanta is coming back tomorrow,' Juan de Pareja said as they used their bread to mop up the last of the soup. 'What will we do about Bartolomé?'

'Maybe she'll have forgotten him,' said Andrés hopefully.

Juan de Pareja shook his head. 'We can't count on that. We have to find a way to set him free.'

They drank their wine in silence for a while.

'I can't think of anything,' said Andrés at last, 'short of asking the Infanta for him.'

'Under no circumstances. That would only make her more determined to hold on to him. A spoilt child like that wants exactly what she knows other people don't want her to have.'

'Don't let anyone hear you talking about the Infanta like that. It could cost you your head,' Andrés warned him, but he was smiling. In this tavern, where only painters met, there were no informers, and the tavern-keeper was well used to his artist guests letting off steam from time to time about the royal household, but there was no real malice in it.

The tavern-keeper, who knew his regular customers well, came to their table now. He bowed gravely to Andrés.

'There's someone at the bar who would like to speak to you.'

'Are you expecting anyone?' asked Juan de Pareja, surprised.

'No.'

Andrés stood up and looked over the heads of the crowd to the bar. He didn't know the man, but the stranger had to be employed at court, since he was wearing the uniform of a royal coachman.

'Send him over,' said Andrés, curious.

Juan stood bashfully in front of Andrés. He didn't know how he should address him. The painter's apprentice was only a young craftsman, but his confident demeanour and the serious, quiet face of the older, carefully dressed man beside him aroused Juan's respect. He gave a slight bow.

'Sir,' said Juan, turning to Andrés, 'please forgive my asking what I am sure is a strange question, but do you know Bartolomé?' Juan faltered. 'He is crippled and a dwarf.'

Andrés banged his fist on the table.

'Do I know him!' he cried. 'It's because of him that we are sitting here racking our brains. We're trying to come up with a plan ...'

Juan de Pareja interrupted him. 'Andrés, I think the coachman wants to ask us something. We should let him speak.'

He pointed to a free chair. 'Sit with us. We'll get the taverner to bring us another jug of wine and a mug.'

He waved at the tavern-keeper and ordered. Juan sat down with the painters. What could Bartolomé have been doing that made this fine gentleman think about him?

'Now, what did you want to ask us?' Andrés looked at Juan with interest.

'I ...' Juan found it difficult to go on. He had never before acknowledged Bartolomé as his son.

'Go on!' said Andrés impatiently.

'I am Bartolomé's father, and I want to take him home.'

'Bartolomé's father!' Andrés leapt up and reached over to shake Juan heartily by the hand. 'Do you know what a talented son you have? You are to be congratulated.'

Juan had no idea what Andrés was talking about. His confusion was so clearly written in his face that Juan de Pareja took pity on him.

'Bartolomé came to us in the studio to be made up by Andrés. He took an interest in our craft, and Andrés allowed him to spend time with us and help out in the studio.'

'I let him paint a picture, and he has talent, great talent. He has the makings of a painter.' Andrés cut the explanation short.

Picture, painter, talent? Juan looked from Andrés' eager face to the quiet, thoughtful face of Juan de Pareja.

'He is a dwarf, a crippled dwarf,' he stammered. They couldn't possibly mean Bartolomé.

Andrés nodded, unperturbed.

'His hands are all right. And so are his eyes and his head. That's all that's required for painting. You must allow us to train him.'

'But a person like him can never be a painter.' It was an absurd idea. The gentlemen must be joking.

Juan de Pareja nodded. 'He can't become a qualified painter. That's correct. The guild would not allow it. But he has talent, and I would be happy to teach him. When he has mastered his craft, he would have no difficulty in getting work in a studio, well-paid work. He could earn his keep and, if he is frugal, he could even save a little.'

Juan was bowled over. He had come here with the hope of finding a way to get Bartolomé back to the village, and here he was, sitting with strangers who were telling him that this crippled child could earn his own money.

Andrés misinterpreted Juan's silence. 'You really must allow him to study with Don Pareja. It's not so important that he can't qualify formally as a painter. Bartolomé understands that, but he wants to paint. Anything is better than this terrible dog's life that he is forced to live at the moment.'

Juan hung his head in shame. Andrés' words pierced him like an accusation.

'There was nothing I could do to defend him. When the Infanta saw Bartolomé on the street, she wanted to have him. I'm just a simple coachman.'

Juan de Pareja put an arm over Juan's shoulder.

'The important thing now is that we find a way together to

get him away from the Infanta,' he said. 'Later, we can take the time to discuss his future.'

'We can't think of anything better,' Andrés admitted freely, 'than to fall on our knees and beg her to let him go.'

'And that is more likely to have the exact opposite effect,' Juan de Pareja added.

The two painters looked at Juan expectantly.

'My family and I have come up with a plan,' said Juan bashfully. 'But in order to make it work we have to make contact with Bartolomé. That's why I came looking for you.'

He explained the plan quickly.

'It might work,' said Juan de Pareja thoughtfully.

'It has to work,' said Andrés. 'I just don't know how.'

'We thought maybe Bartolomé should make a present of the little dog to the Infanta, and then ask her to let him go,' said Juan.

'She won't agree to that,' replied Juan de Pareja. 'She'll want to keep both of them.'

'It'll have to be like magic,' murmured Andrés.

'What do you mean, magic?'

'Magic. Bartolomé disappears and the dog shows up. Then the Infanta will think that Bartolomé has been changed into a real dog.'

'But that's impossible,' said Juan.

Juan de Pareja thought for a while. The solution was getting closer. He must just … He smiled. He was remembering his trip to Rome with Velázquez.

'This magic can happen,' he said confidently.

The Magician
and his Trick

NICOLASITO PERTUSATO was the reluctant focus of a small group that had gathered in the painters' studio.

Juan de Pareja, dressed in dark colours and serious as ever, Andrés in his stained painter's smock and Léon were standing around the vain little creature, who was all dickied up. Bartolomé was sitting a little to the side, on the cold marble flagstones. He had Justo in his arms. His father had handed the dog over to Andrés that morning outside the palace.

Bartolomé was stroking the little dog tenderly. If it all worked out, it would be taking his place at the Infanta's side in a matter of hours. Then he would be free to start a new life.

Juan de Pareja had spoken to Bartolomé's father and they had made the arrangements. He was going to be allowed to stay in Madrid. As Joaquín lived with the baker, he was going to live with the painters. He would be able to come home on visits from time to time, and one day, he would give his father a few coins from his first pay packet. He would never have thought it possible that it could have worked out like this.

The little dog rubbed his soft snout against Bartolomé's arm. 'She will definitely be fond of you,' the dwarf promised him. The puppy licked Bartolomé's hand with his red tongue.

'If she hurts you,' the dwarf whispered earnestly, 'you can bite her, do you hear? She's really only a little girl and she has no right to mess you about. You have to watch out for yourself. If she kicks you out, then you can come to me in the studio. I'll hide you.'

Bartolomé hugged the puppy close.

Juan de Pareja's strong voice came through loud and clear. 'Nicolasito, you are the only one who has the skill for this,' Juan de Pareja was explaining earnestly.

Nicolasito gave an arrogant nod. 'I know. But why should I do it? What's in it for me?'

Bartolomé's confident mood vanished. Of course Nicolasito had no interest in helping him. Why would he? The worse things were for him, the more pleased the page was.

'Just think!' Andrés urged him. What he'd really like to do, though he would never say it aloud, would be to give the silly dwarf in his page costume a clip on the ear. *Is it not enough*, he wanted to shout, *that you can help Bartolomé to start a new life?*

Nicolasito's eyes were glittering. He felt his power, and he was enjoying it.

Juan de Pareja laid a soothing hand on Andrés' shoulder. Andrés did not finish his sentence. He stared furiously at Nicolasito. Nicolasito smiled.

Juan de Pareja picked up where Andrés had left off. He spoke thoughtfully.

'The lady-in-waiting Maria Augustina de Sarmiento would be very annoyed if you outwitted her. She has not got a high opinion of dwarves. I once heard her calling you the Infanta's dolly.'

Bartolomé pricked up his ears. Nicolasito – a doll, a plaything? Had all that talk of friendship just been bravado?

'That's not true, you're lying!' cried Nicolasito. His pretty face was fiery red.

'I heard that too,' Léon chipped in. 'You should pay her back. And now you have a once-in-a-lifetime opportunity.'

Nicolasito thought it over. If he went along with the painters' plan he could get one over on the lady-in-waiting. In the Infanta's eyes, he would be the greatest, and if he played his cards right, he could ... An enchanting dream began to play itself out before Nicolasito's eyes. He could make Maria Augustina de Sarmiento the laughing stock of the court. If the Infanta was on his side, then the lady-in-waiting wouldn't have a chance of defending herself.

On the other hand, it irritated him that Bartolomé, of all people, would gain his freedom through this plan. How in the world had the cripple managed to gain the obvious attention and favour of the painters? Enviously, he looked over at Bartolomé. Nobody had ever put themselves out for *him*.

Juan de Pareja must have sensed Nicolasito's negative feelings.

'This magic trick has never before been performed in a European court,' he lied. 'It comes from the east and is the best-guarded secret of the magicians there.'

In reality, he had seen the trick in the court of an Italian count and had persuaded the magician, on a whim, to show him how it was done. It was a simple but clever mechanism that, together with two mirrors, made the trick work. In return, he had painted a portrait of the magician.

'If he hasn't got the nerve for it, then I'll do it,' Andrés added angrily.

Juan de Pareja shook his head.

'The trick depends on sleight-of-hand. Only a person who

has mastered that to perfection will succeed in it.'

Nicolasito wavered. Juan de Pareja's words flattered him.

Suddenly he grinned. Of course he would agree. Wouldn't it give him the power to reveal how the trick worked at a later stage, whenever he felt like it, and so force Bartolomé to be a human dog once again?

Juan de Pareja could see what was behind Nicolasito's sly smile. But once Bartolomé had been turned into a proper dog, in full view of the Infanta, he would be able to protect the boy from any more cruelties Nicolasito might have in store for him.

'Agreed,' said Nicolasito.

Bartolomé gave a sigh of relief. Nicolasito was the right choice. Once the Infanta's favourite dwarf had declared himself ready to help, then he was very keen to make sure that the performance of which he was to be the star was properly organised. He gave orders, demanded a cloak of black velvet and secretly had his face made up.

They were all ready when the Infanta's coach drove into the palace courtyard late in the afternoon. Nicolasito was waiting for her there. Bartolomé hunkered next to him, dressed as a dog. Behind them stood a large wooden crate, painted with strange characters and symbols.

'Real Arabian magic formulas,' Juan de Pareja had explained to Nicolasito.

'Nonsense, we painted whatever we felt like,' whispered Andrés to Bartolomé. 'Juan hasn't got a word of Arabic. He came to Europe as a child.'

In the crate, in a compartment hidden behind a mirror, was Justo. From outside the box, Bartolomé was talking reassuringly to him. The little dog was not to be scared of the dark.

Andrés, Léon and Juan de Pareja had also changed their clothes. They were wearing long white robes and were standing humbly behind Nicolasito.

The Infanta allowed herself to be lifted from the coach by Don Nieto, her chamberlain. She was tired and cranky after the hot, bumpy journey.

Doña de Sarmiento, equally exhausted and sweating, followed her. When she saw the absurdly dressed Nicolasito, she raised her eyebrows disapprovingly. What was he thinking of to approach the Infanta like this? She wanted to get rid of him, but Nicolasito was ahead of her. He pranced up to the Infanta and gave an exaggerated bow.

'Greetings, my Infanta. I am the Great Wizard of the Far East and I bring you the most amazing magic, to cheer up my Infanta after her ...' Nicolasito could not refrain from throwing a meaningful look at the lady-in-waiting, who was standing by the carriage in her crumpled travelling dress. '... after your extremely boring journey, which you have had to undertake without the benefit of my company.'

The little Infanta smiled. Her tiredness was forgotten and her bad mood had disappeared. Intrigued, she looked at her page from the arms of her chamberlain.

'I am going to perform the greatest magic trick of all time for my Infanta!' boasted Nicolasito.

The little girl clapped her hands delightedly. With a sweeping arm movement, Nicolasito pointed at Bartolomé and the crate.

'*Entero magis Labyrinthum.*'

Obediently, Bartolomé sat up and begged for the last time. The Infanta took hardly any notice of him. She was too absorbed in anticipation of the promised trick.

Andrés came forward hastily and opened the little door of the wooden crate.

'This crate is totally empty,' whispered Nicolasito in a dark voice. Out of the folds of his velvet cloak, he took a magic wand and he made circles in the air in front of the opening.

Bartolomé crawled into the crate. Andrés closed the trapdoor. The Infanta had escaped from the arms of her chamberlain and, standing on the ground, was watching the performance open-mouthed. Nicolasito made mysterious movements with his wand and murmured the magic words that he had invented himself, in a language also of his own invention. Andrés, Léon and Juan de Pareja turned the crate a couple of times in a circle so that the wooden boards clattered loudly on the cobblestones. In this way, any sound from the crate would be disguised.

Inside the box, Bartolomé opened the hidden trapdoor and changed places with the puppy. Justo licked Bartolomé's face in delight.

'Stop that,' Bartolomé reprimanded the puppy. 'You must keep very quiet and don't bark.' He shut the trapdoor carefully again, and the mirrors slipped back into place.

At that very moment, the turning stopped.

Outside, the painters took a step back and bowed to Nicolasito, who stepped up to the crate, and, with a single movement of his hand, yanked open the little door. The little dog blinked, startled, in the bright sunlight. In front of it, it could see the outline of a little girl.

'A dog,' yelled the child in a high voice.

Justo did what he had been taught to do. He ran to the girl and leapt up at her in excitement. The Infanta went down on her knees and stretched out her arms.

Justo hopped into them, barked in his soft doggy voice and pressed his funny little snout to the royal cheek. He took the heart of the Infanta by storm.

Nicolasito stood gravely by, assured of the princess's gratitude. Maria Augustina de Sarmiento gathered her skirts together and hurried away. Nobody noticed Andrés, Juan de Pareja and Léon carrying the crate with Bartolomé in it quickly into the palace.

Upstairs, at the tall window of the studio, stood Don Velázquez, watching the events below in the courtyard. He would change his masterpiece once again, he decided, with a sudden burst of inspiration. Instead of the king's hound, he would paint in the Infanta's new dog. Not as a little puppy, but fully grown. When he was older, Justo would be a fine dog with a thick, gleaming, golden-brown coat.

Don Velázquez started to scrape off the half-dried layers of paint. Underneath, the outline of the original drawing started to show through. He didn't notice Juan de Pareja coming into the studio with Bartolomé in his arms. They came and stood behind him.

'Why?' Bartolomé dared to ask the famous court painter when he saw the picture.

Don Velázquez leapt up, startled, turned around and looked into Bartolomé's anxious face.

'I'm not going to paint *you*,' he assured the dwarf. 'I'm going to paint Justo, as he will be one day, in your place.'

Bartolomé let out a sigh of relief.

'And you will get down to work and mix the appropriate paints,' Don Velázquez continued. 'But of course,' he turned to Juan de Pareja, 'only if your own master allows you,' he said politely and with an emphasis that Juan de Pareja fully understood.

The Moorish painter, who would never be a master, did not flinch. 'I am a student myself and always will be. Whatever my esteemed master suggests, I can only act on it, and anyone who wants to study with me will do the same,' he promised quietly.

Don Velázquez nodded, satisfied. It was right that Juan de Pareja knew his place, and would train Bartolomé to take his place also.

Bartolomé didn't care about all that. The main thing was that he was going to be allowed to learn to paint. Carefully, he chose a suitable shade from the great selection of pigments.

Through the open window came Nicolasito's voice, prompting Justo to show off his tricks. The Infanta clapped her hands and her laugh echoed across the courtyard.

Never again, thought Bartolomé, bending over the grinding glass and starting eagerly to grind the brown powder.